PRIVATE RILEY

A TIME TRAVEL ADVENTURE

VICTORIA RUSH

VOLUME 3

RILEY'S TIME TRAVEL ADVENTURES -
BOOK 3

COPYRIGHT

ALSO BY VICTORIA RUSH

Adult Fairytales:

The Enchanted Forest: An Erotic Fairytale

The Land of Giants: An Erotic Fairytale

The Dragon's Lair: An Erotic Fairytale

Witch's Brew: An Erotic Fairytale

The Mage's Spell: An Erotic Fairytale

The Mermaid Lagoon: An Erotic Fairytale

The Coven: An Erotic Fairytale

Rapunzel: An Erotic Fairytale

The Seven Dwarfs: An Erotic Fairytale

The Land of Mutants: An Erotic Fairytale

The Erotic Temple: A Sexy Fairytale (Coming Soon)

Erotica Themed Bundles:

Voyeur: Lesbian Erotica Bundle

Public Affairs: A Lesbian Anthology

Futa Fantasies: The Ladyboy Collection

Threesomes: The Lesbian Collection

Threesomes - Volume 2: The Lesbian Collection

First Time: A Lesbian Anthology

Hedonism: An Erotic Anthology

Switch Hitters: Bisexual Erotica

Taboo Erotica: The Lesbian Series

BDSM: The Lesbian Collection

Party Games: The Erotic Collection

Party Games 2: The Erotic Collection

All Girl 1: Lesbian Erotica Bundle

All Girl 2: Lesbian Erotica Bundle

All Girl 3: Lesbian Erotica Bundle

All Girl 4: Lesbian Erotica Bundle

Erotic Fairytale Bundles:

Clover's Fantasy Adventures: Books 1 - 5

Clover's Fantasy Adventures: Books 6 - 10

Erotic Fantasy:

Pirate's Bounty: A Time Travel Adventure

Wild West: A Time Travel Adventure

Private Riley: A Time Travel Adventure

Cleopatra's Secret: A Time Travel Adventure

Bounty Hunter 2125: A Time Travel Adventure

Ninja Assassin: A Time Travel Adventure

The 300: A Time Travel Adventure

Arabian Nights: An Erotic Fairytale (coming soon...)

Steamy Time Travel Bundles:

Riley's Time Travel Adventures: Books 1 - 5

Lesbian Erotica:

The Dinner Party: Lesbian Voyeur Erotica

The Darkroom: Bisexual Voyeur Erotica

Naked Yoga: Lesbian Transgender Erotica

Nude Cruise: Bisexual Voyeur Erotica

Rush Hour: Taboo Public Sex

The Girl Next Door: First Time Lesbian Erotic Romance

Girls' Camp: Lesbian Group Sex

Wet Dream: Ladyboy Fantasy Erotica

The Convent: Taboo Sex with a Nun

Sex Robot: A Dream Sex Machine

The Personal Trainer: Getting Pumped at the Gym

The Dominatrix: BDSM Lesbian Domination

Webcam Chat: Lesbian Online Sex

Paint Me: A Kinky Bodypainting Workshop

The Toy Party: Girls Sharing Sex Toys

The Costume Party: Strapping One On

Swedish Sauna: Lesbian Group Sex

The Therapist: Taboo Lesbian Erotica

Elevator Shaft: Bisexual Threesomes Erotica

Ladyboy: Lesbian Transgender Erotica

Peep Show: Lesbian Voyeur Erotica

The Dare: Public Sex Erotica

Maid Service: Lesbian Threesomes Erotica

The Hitchhiker: First Time Lesbian Erotica

The Housesitter: Spycam Lesbian Erotica

The Spa: Lesbian Group Orgy

Parlor Games: Blindfold Sex Party

The Exchange Student: First Time Lesbian Erotica

The Hostel: Bisexual Group Erotica

The Harem: Lesbian Erotic Romance

The Orient Express: Lesbian Voyeur Erotica

The First Lady: A Forbidden Lesbian Erotic Romance

The Slave: Lesbian BDSM Erotica

The Masseuse: Lesbian Sensuous Erotica

Too Close for Comfort: Lesbian Forbidden Erotica

Naked Twister: A Wild Party Game

Lexi: The Sex App (Lesbian Fantasy Erotica)

Call Girl: Lesbian Bisexual Threesomes Erotica

Circle Jill: Lesbian Masturbation Workshop

The Viewing Room: Masturbation Voyeur Erotica

Spin the Bottle: A Kinky Party Game

The Hair Salon: Lesbian Voyeur Erotica

Tribadism 1: Girls Only Sex Workshop

Tribadism 2: The Art of Scissoring

Tribadism 3: Threeway Hookups

The Kiss: A Game of Oral Sex

Pledge Week: Sorority Sisters

Carny Games 1: A Wild Sex Party

Carny Games 2: A Kinky Sex Party

Carny Games 3: An Erotic Sex Party

Dreamscape: An Artificial Reality Game

Glory Hole: Guess Who's On the Other Side

Joy Ride: A Late Night Erotic Bus Trip

The Blind Girl: An Erotic Romance(Coming Soon)

Lesbian Erotica Bundles:

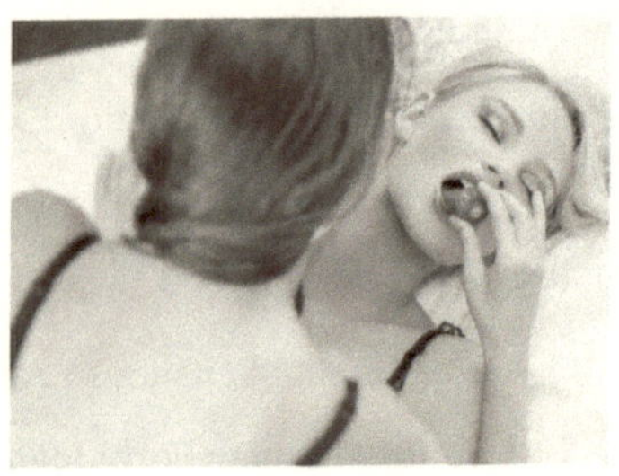

Jade's Erotic Adventures: Books 1 - 5

Jade's Erotic Adventures: Books 6 - 10

Jade's Erotic Adventures: Books 11 - 15

Jade's Erotic Adventures: Books 16 - 20

Jade's Erotic Adventures: Books 21 - 25

Jade's Erotic Adventures: Books 26 - 30

Standalone Stories:

The Polynesian Girl: A Lesbian EroticRomance

For the uninhibited...

WANT TO AMP UP YOUR SEX LIFE?

Sign up for my newsletter to receive more free books and other steamy stuff. Discover a hundred different ways to wet your whistle!

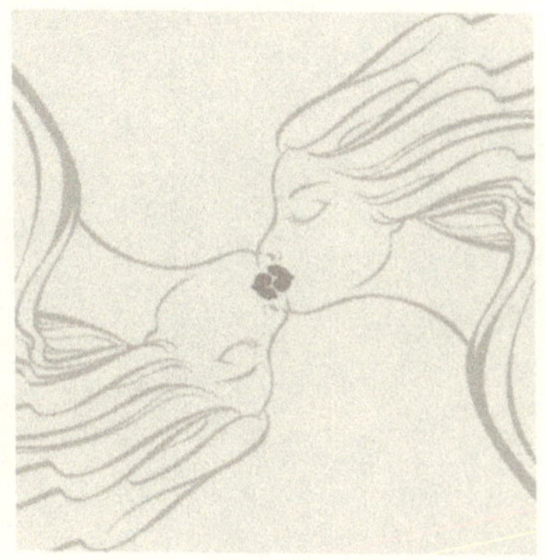

Victoria Rush Erotica

1

Riley tiptoed down the stairs then untied her horse from the hitching post in front of the saloon, trotting her horse slowly down the main street. When she reached the outskirts of Cody, she dismounted and slapped the animal's behind, sending it back in the direction of town.

Then she pulled her time travel device from her back pocket, tapping the screen. The familiar funnel began to swirl over the glass, and as it began to rise up in a three-dimensional vortex, she looked back at the saloon in the distance, noticing a dim light in Bess's room, with the curtains pulled to the side. While she raised her hand to say goodbye to her friends, she felt herself pulled into the funnel, tumbling through the portal once again, unsure where she'd land.

When she fell into the middle of a pitch-black field, she peered up, noticing loud explosions overhead. As she knelt in the grass trying to get her bearings, an enormous steel tank rolled past her with a swastika emblazoned on the side.

Jesus, she muttered to herself. *Why do I always have to end up in the middle of a conflict?*

Suddenly, a G.I. wearing a U.S. army helmet pulled up beside her, dragging her back down into the grass.

"What in God's name are you doing in the middle of no-man's-land?" the soldier said, squinting his eyes at Riley's uniform. "And what are you doing wearing a cowboy hat and a Colt 45?"

"It's complicated," Riley sighed, realizing she'd gotten herself into a whole heap of new trouble.

"Well, keep your head down while we head back to our base. It'll be safer for you there. This is no place for a girl to be playing dress-up."

While the duo crawled through the grass, bullets flew over their heads as soldiers scurried about in every direction, picking off enemy combatants like some kind of frenetic paintball game. Except this was no game, and the red splotches exploding on the chests of the fighting soldiers wasn't paint.

"Where are we?" Riley whispered as she listened to the sound of stomping boots around them.

"You're in Ardennes, France, with the U.S. Second Army," the G.I. said, peering anxiously around him. "Although right now, I'm not sure whether you're on the American or German side of the front line."

Ardennes, Riley thought. She'd studied WWII history in high school and remembered that was where the brutal Battle of the Bulge had been fought.

"What time is it?" she said.

"Seriously?" the G.I. said, peering at her with a furrowed brow. "You're in the middle of a major battle and you want to know what time it is?"

"Not so much the time, as the *year*. More importantly, the month."

"All this shelling must have really jolted your memory," the G.I. said. "It's December, 1944."

Riley scrunched her face, trying to remember the details of the decisive battle that turned the tide of the war. Suddenly, she remembered the date of the huge German counteroffensive: December 16.

"What day?"

"Jesus," the G.I. said, shaking his head. "The last time I checked, it was December 13. Although in the heat of the battle, I've kind of lost track of when the clock ticked past midnight."

"Can you take me to the headquarters of your commanding officer?" Riley said. "I've got some important information he'll want to know."

"Let's get you to the base camp first," the G.I. said, ducking another bullet. "Then we'll worry about getting you in front of the right brass. I'm pretty sure my C.O. will be just as interested as I am knowing how you managed to infiltrate this far into the front lines wearing not much more than a cowboy hat."

Suddenly, a German soldier lunged at the G.I. with his bayonet and the corporal stumbled onto his back, trying to evade the spear. As the soldier raised his rifle to shoot the stricken G.I., Riley pulled her revolver out of her holster and shot the soldier in the chest, sending him flying in the opposite direction. Within seconds, three more German soldiers materialized from the tall grass, and Riley whirled around, picking them off one-by-one with her six-shooter.

"Holy shit!" the G.I. said with wide eyes. "Where did you learn to shoot like that?"

"I had a little target practice back at the range," Riley

said, looking around nervously. "But never with this many bad guys around. We better get out of here before we run out of ammo."

"Good idea," the G.I. said, holding his hand over his eyes and peering into the distance. "Our camp is only a few hundred yards away. Can you run in those boots?"

"Something tells me we're about to find out," Riley nodded.

The G.I. grabbed her hand, then the two of them stood up and raced through the grass with shells exploding beside them until they reached a fortified bunker surrounded with sandbags, leaping over the wall and falling into a dusty trench.

"What the hell, Johnson?" a military officer with two bars on his collar said, approaching the couple. "Why aren't you out there fighting with your platoon?"

"I found this woman wandering around in a daze and brought her here for safety," the G.I. said.

The officer peered at Riley in her strange western garb and held out his hand to help her up. He was tall and ruggedly handsome, only a few years older than Riley, and she smiled as he pulled her to her feet.

"What's your name, ma'am?" the officer said. "And what in God's name are you doing in the middle of this battle?"

"It's a little hard to explain," Riley said, dusting off her vest and leather chaps. She knew no one would believe her story of being transported back in time via a time machine. "Let's just say I fell into it accidentally."

"Accidentally?" the officer said, peering at her strange clothes. "Is that a *sheriff's* badge you're wearing?"

"Yes," Riley said, suddenly wishing she'd changed into less obvious clothes before leaving Cody. "Like I said, it's a bit complicated."

"Where are you from?" he said, glancing down at her open V-neck shirt.

"Boston," Riley said. "By way of Cody."

"Wyoming?" the officer said, widening his eyes. "How the hell did you get all the way out here and past the front lines?"

"I don't have time to explain right now. I need to see your C.O. to warn him about an impending enemy offensive. It's going to be the biggest one of the war and if you don't prepare properly, thousands of lives will be lost."

"And you know this *how* exactly?" the officer said, crossing his arms over his chest. "Why should I believe a teenager wearing a cowboy costume?"

Riley peered at the officer's heavily muscled arms and broad shoulders, barely concealed by his tight-fitting uniform.

"I know a lot more than you can imagine," she huffed. "I can tell you how many U.S. troops are in France, and who is exactly where on the battlefield, on both sides."

"How could you possibly know that?" the young officer said, squinting at Riley's sweaty cleavage in her checkered shirt under her leather vest.

"You're just going to have to take my word for it," Riley said, feeling her face becoming flushed from the combination of anger at the officer's petulant tone and his hunky appearance. "In the meantime, you can use my skills. I know how to handle a gun, and I'm not afraid to use it."

The officer paused for a moment, peering down at the old-fashioned revolver resting in her holster at her side.

"It's true, captain," the G.I. nodded. "She's a dead aim. She took down four Krauts while we made our way back here."

"I don't know what your story is, sweetheart," the officer

said, staring Riley in the eye. "The C.O. is likely to have even less patience than me for tolerating little girls in costume near the front line. But we need to get you away from the front lines, and command HQ is as good a place as any."

"Would you like me to drive her, captain?" the G.I. said.

"No," the captain smiled, running his eyes over Riley's curvy figure. "I think this shipment needs special handling."

2

———

An hour later, Riley's jeep rolled into the main square of Bastogne, skidding to a stop in front of the town hall. Captain Miller stepped out of the vehicle and led her up the front steps, past the receptionist, into a large corner office. A man with a buzz cut and silver sideburns looked up from behind his desk and coughed when he saw Riley's outfit.

"Jesus, you weren't kidding when you said you found a girl in a cowboy outfit, Jim," he said, pushing some maps to the side of his desk and leaning back in his chair. "What's your story, darling? What the hell are you doing in the middle of a world war wearing not much more than a Colt 45?"

"You wouldn't believe me if I told you," Riley said. "The important thing is that I have important information that can turn the course of the war."

"*Really* now?" the colonel said, grinning in the captain's direction. "And what might that be, exactly?"

"The Germans are going to mount a massive counter-invasion in the Ardennes Forest three days from now. If you don't move enough troops there to meet the attack, your army will be pushed back a hundred miles and thousands of allied troops will be lost."

The colonel peered at Riley with an incredulous look, then he pushed his chair back from his desk, crossing his feet over the table.

"Huh," he chuckled, looking at the captain like Riley was some kind of alien. "And how did you come upon this critical piece of intelligence, exactly? Did you just walk over the enemy lines and ask their commander?"

"No," Riley said, crossing her arms over her chest. "I acquired it through other means."

"Other means," the colonel said, raising his eyebrows. "Do tell."

"It's classified," Riley said, not knowing how else to explain her unusual circumstances. "I'm not at liberty to say."

"So you expect me to believe that a teenage girl dressed up in a cowboy costume has detailed knowledge of enemy troop movements and plans that even our highest levels of command doesn't know?"

"Yes."

The colonel paused for a moment while he appraised Riley's tight figure, then he stopped, peering into her eyes with a steely gaze.

"My patience is wearing thin, young lady," he said. "I'll give you exactly one more minute to explain yourself. *Prove* it."

Riley stepped toward the colonel's desk, turning around one of his maps. Then she pointed her finger toward the northern coast of France, tapping her finger along the coastline.

"The allied forces landed one hundred and sixty thousand troops on the beaches of Normandy on D-Day. U.S. troops landed on Utah and Omaha beaches, the British on Gold and Sword, and the Canadians on Juno."

"Just about everybody knows that by now," the colonel huffed. "That information has already been widely disseminated by the western papers. And it wasn't named D-Day until after the fact. Only the top brass knows the official name of the operation."

"You mean *Operation Overlord*?" Riley said, placing her hands on her hips.

The colonel's expression suddenly turned serious as his eyes darted toward the captain, who was standing beside Riley, trying to hold back a grin.

"That wouldn't be hard to know if you knew the right people," the colonel said. "I'm sure a comely lass like you could easily get into a commander's pants with a bit of subterfuge."

"Would a comely lass like me know that the German Second Army has fifty thousand troops and three Panzer divisions poised on the other side of your enemy line?"

The colonel glanced at his map, then back up at Riley.

"How could you possibly know that?" he said, standing up slowly.

"Let's just say that I've got some special connections."

"Are you going to share these special connections with us?"

"I'm not sure you're the best one to share my intelligence with," Riley said. "After all, you're just a colonel. You're only in charge of a regiment, at best. I need to speak with the commander of the U.S. First Army."

"Why you little–" the colonel said, stepping around his desk to face Riley directly. "I could have you thrown in the brig as a spy. Why would I ever let you have an audience with a four-star general?"

"Because if you don't, you'll have to answer for the loss of thousands of allied lives. Not to mention your own headquarters will be overrun in days if you don't. Do you really want to explain how a little girl knew more than you did about the biggest battle of the war?"

The colonel paused for a long moment as his eyes darted between the stoic captain standing by his side and the maps strewn over his desk. After a few minutes, he looked up.

"You've got balls, I'll give you that," he said. "We'll keep an eye on enemy movements over the next forty-eight hours, and if your predictions come true, I'll turn you over to Central Command."

He peered over at the captain and nodded.

"In the meantime, you'll stay here under the watchful eye of the captain. You better hope you're right about all this, otherwise you'll be in a hell of a lot more trouble for distracting our military planners in the middle of an important campaign."

"It'll be my pleasure," Riley said, smiling at the handsome captain. "But you better not wait too long. The Germans will be knocking on our doorstep in a matter of days."

3

———————

After the colonel dismissed Captain Miller and Riley from his office, the captain escorted Riley down a long corridor, opening the door to a spartan room with a single cot.

"This will be your living quarters for the next forty-eight hours," he said, motioning for her to enter the room.

"Am I free to come and go as I please?" Riley said, noticing the wire-mesh glass window.

"Only in this wing of the headquarters," the captain nodded. "There's a unisex lavatory at the end of the hall and a mess hall around the corner."

"Where will you be all this time?"

"In the room right next to you. The colonel's asked me to keep a close eye on you, and that's what I intend to do."

"Do you have laundry or any other services in this place? How am I supposed to keep myself entertained in this dungeon for two full days?"

"I'll bring you a fresh change of clothes in a little while," the captain said. "In the meantime, I'll have to take your weapon for safekeeping."

"What if the Germans invade?" Riley said, unhappy to hand over her only form of self-defense. "How will I protect myself?"

"That remains to be determined. But you'll be safe under my care. I won't let anything happen to you."

"Fair enough," Riley said, pulling her pistol out of her holster and handing it to the captain, handle first.

"Thanks," he said. "If you need anything else, feel free to tap on my door anytime.

"I'll do that," Riley nodded, suddenly conscious of the dampness in her panties as she peered back at the handsome officer.

After the captain disappeared down the hall, Riley went to the lavatory to relieve herself, then she returned to her room, removing her chaps and cowboy boots to massage her aching feet. A few minutes later, there was a soft tap on her door, and when she opened it, the captain was standing in the hall holding some neatly pressed clothes.

"All I could scrounge up was a woman's army uniform," he said. "I had to guess your size, so I hope it fits."

He glanced down at Riley's bare feet, then he peered up.

"I brought you some patent dress shoes instead of boots, since I thought they were more befitting a lady. I can't imagine you'll be going anywhere near the front lines again anytime soon."

"Thanks," Riley said, holding out her arms as the captain passed her the clothes. "I'm sure they'll be fine."

"Was there anything else you needed?" the captain said, hesitating by the door.

"Um..." Riley stammered, staring at the captain's muscular shoulders.

For a moment, she considered asking him into her room, remembering how much she missed the feeling of a man's hard body and cock pressing against her. But she didn't want to appear too forward, unsure of the protocol in this era.

"I could definitely go for a bite to eat," she said. "All this excitement has worked up an appetite. Can you show me the way to the mess hall?"

"I'll be happy to accompany you," the captain nodded. "It's probably best that I don't let you out of my sight for very long. The colonel would have my head if you disappeared on my watch."

"Well we wouldn't want you losing such a pretty head," Riley smiled. "Give me a few minutes to change and I'll join you shortly."

After Riley changed into her new clothes and hid her time machine, she opened the door, where the captain was leaning against the adjacent wall waiting for her. He peered at her neatly pressed military fatigues clinging tightly to her body and nodded approvingly.

"Do the clothes fit alright?" he asked.

"They're a little snug for my frame," Riley said. "I've barely got enough room to breathe. But something tells me you planned it that way."

"I wouldn't think of it," the captain smiled. "I can always get you a larger size if you prefer."

"I imagine these will stretch over time," Riley said, happy to flaunt her athletic figure in the presence of the hunky officer. "As long as there's enough room to fit some extra food in my belly."

When Riley and the captain entered the mess hall, they lined up at the cafeteria-style counter, receiving two plate-fuls of shepherd's pie and green beans, then they found a table in the corner of the room to eat their food.

"So what's *your* story?" Riley said, gulping down her steaming dinner. "How did you end up in this big mess of a war?"

"I could have avoided the draft, since I was in college at the time," the captain nodded. "But I wanted to serve my country and do my part to fight the Nazi menace."

"Yeah, it's pretty horrific," Riley said, noticing the colonel sitting with a group of other high-ranking officers on the other side of the mess hall. "But the good guys win in the end."

"How can you be so sure?"

"The Russians are pressing in from the east, Patton's army is rapidly reclaiming territory in the south, and the Normandy landing force is making daily gains moving from the west. It's only a matter of time before Hitler's Wehrmacht is defeated."

"You seem to know an awful lot about the war for someone so young."

"I'm a keen observer of current events, what can I say?"

"It appears that you're a lot more than that," the captain said. "You have knowledge of troop movements that only someone close to the top brass would have."

"Are you suggesting that I'm sleeping with the enemy, like the colonel suggested?"

"Of course not. It's just that–"

"What about you?" Riley said, eager to learn more about

the handsome captain. "Is there a special someone waiting for *you* back home?"

"If you mean a girlfriend, no," the captain said. "I hardly had time between my studies then my enlistment in the army."

"It'll be a few more years before women are allowed to join combat troops," Riley nodded. "It must get pretty lonely up there on the front lines."

"Women are the last thing I'm thinking about when shells are exploding all around us. I've got to stay focused on defeating the enemy before I begin thinking about such leisurely pursuits."

"But you do like *girls*, don't you?" Riley said, watching the captain's arm muscles flexing in his shirt as he lifted his fork to his mouth. "I'm mean, you're not–"

"God, no," he said. "I'm definitely an admirer of the fairer sex."

"Thank heavens," Riley smiled. "Because it would be a waste to let all that prime beef go to waste."

4

———

After dinner, Riley and the captain returned to their quarters, with the two of them lingering at her door while they bade each other good night. It took all of her willpower not to drag him into her dorm room, but she didn't want to risk damaging what little credibility she still held in the colonel's eyes before she had a chance to pass along her knowledge of the impending German troop movements.

As she lay down on her cot, she thought about the handsome captain and what he'd said about his lonely life on the front lines. She felt sorry for him, but more than that, she felt incredibly turned on by his brave yet innocent demeanor. There was something incredibly sexy about his strong, unassuming manner that she hadn't witnessed in a long time.

As she pulled off her pants and bunched them around her ankles, she slipped her fingers under her panties, imagining what it would be like to feel his rippling muscles pressing against her. Before long, her juices were dripping down the insides of her thighs as she moaned softly, succumbing to the rising pleasure emanating from her hips.

Suddenly, she heard an unusual squeaking sound coming from the other side of the wall, and she paused, holding her breath. The sound had a regular cadence to it, and as the squeaking grew louder and faster, she realized that the handsome captain was pleasuring himself only a few inches away.

Holy shit, she thought, thrusting three fingers into her sopping pussy. *Should I knock on the wall to signal for him to come over here? The poor guy probably hasn't been laid in months. And I'd far rather have a throbbing cock in my peachka than my skinny little fingers.*

But she resisted the temptation, opting instead to listen to the sound of his soft grunting and breathing as the bed squeaking ramped up in volume. When it finally stopped, Riley held her breath, straining to listen to the sound of his heaving as he struggled to regain his breath after climaxing.

"Fuck me," Riley grunted, driving her fingers in and out of her pussy as she lifted her hips off the mattress, nearing her own climax.

Suddenly, she heard the sound of the captain's door opening and his footsteps receding down the hall in the direction of the lavatory. She got out of bed and opened her door a crack, waiting for him to return. When he exited the lavatory, she could see the bulge in his pants as he adjusted himself and walked awkwardly back in the direction of his room. Riley closed her door and waited until his footfalls approached her room, then she suddenly swung open the door, grabbing the captain by his lapels and pulling him into her room.

"What the–?" he said, bulging his eyes in surprise.

Riley swung him against the back of her door, pulling

his face toward her lips and kissing him passionately while he pretended to protest.

"We shouldn't be doing this..." he said, pulling away temporarily. "If the colonel finds out, we could both get in a lot of trouble."

"What's the worst he could do?" Riley said, pulling him close to her body as she lifted her right thigh over his hips. "Throw us in the stockade and accuse us of unseemly behavior? Surely you're not the first soldier to avail himself of the services of a lonely girl during a break away from the front lines?"

"Yes, but–"

"I heard what you were doing in your room a few minutes ago," Riley smiled, placing his left hand over her raised thigh. "Wouldn't you rather feel the soft skin of a woman than the rough callouses of your own hand?"

"Oh God," the captain murmured, sliding his hand up Riley's thigh and caressing the curvature of her hips.

"Do you think you still have some fuel in the tank?" Riley purred, grabbing the captain's swollen member and squeezing his balls softly.

"This cannon's got plenty more ammo in the turret," he nodded, dragging Riley over to the bed.

When they fell onto the cot, the captain tore Riley's underwear, pulling it off her legs, then he hiked her knees up to her chest, unzipping his trousers while he fished his engorged cock out of his pants. When he rammed his erection into her hole, Riley gasped at his size. Easily one of the largest pricks she'd ever experienced, she wrapped her legs around his powerful hips while he slid her body up and down on the bed, creating a loud grinding sound as the metal frame strained under their combined weight.

So much for his sweet, innocent disguise, Riley thought as the strapping captain banged her against the squeaking bedsprings. It didn't take her long to reach orgasm, and when she bit his ear with her muffled cries, he grunted loudly, emptying his load inside her.

"Holy fuck," Riley panted, holding on to him with her nails still digging into his back. "Where have you been all my life? And how could you possibly hold back those talents all this time?"

"I guess I just haven't had the right opportunity to exercise them," he smiled, rolling off her onto the side. "I haven't had a pretty girl like you cross my path for quite some time now."

"Well, I think we should try to make the best use of our short time together while the colonel decides what he wants to do with me."

"Works for me," the captain said, caressing Riley's quivering tummy.

Suddenly, there was a loud knock on the door and the two lovers peered at one another with wide eyes.

"Who is it?" Riley said, pulling on her pants hastily.

"Major Wilson, ma'am," and man's voice returned. "The colonel would like to speak with you in his quarters."

"Just a moment, please," Riley said, motioning for the captain to hide behind the dresser on the opposite wall.

She straightened her hair in the mirror over the dresser, then calmly opened the door, trying her best to look unfazed.

"Tell him I'll be there in a few minutes," she said, pressing her hands over the wrinkles in her uniform. "I just need a few moments to put myself together."

"Alright, but please don't delay," the major said. "The colonel's a busy man."

"Of course," Riley nodded.

"I don't suppose you've seen Captain Miller around?" the major said. "He's not answering his door, and I can't find him anywhere in the building."

"I haven't a clue," Riley said with a straight face. "Ever since lunch time, he's been persona non grata."

"Please let us know if you see him," the major said. "The colonel has a separate matter to discuss with him."

"Of course," Riley said, closing the door and wheeling around to peer at the captain with bulging eyes.

5

After Riley and Captain Miller composed themselves, they walked to the colonel's office together, presenting themselves at his open door. There was another officer seated on the sofa in the corner of the room, and he peered at the couple suspiciously. The colonel looked up from some papers he was reading on his desk and removed his glasses.

"Where the hell have you been, Miller?" he said. "We haven't been able to find you anywhere for the last half hour."

"I was in the lavatory," the captain lied, unable to come up with a better excuse on such short notice.

"For half an hour?"

"I guess my dinner didn't agree with me," he said, rubbing his stomach.

The colonel paused as his eyes darted between Riley and the captain, inspecting their flush faces.

"Well, you're here now, so have a seat. Both of you. There's something we need to discuss."

The couple sat in the armchairs on the other side of the colonel's desk, glancing at one another nervously.

"Your intel about German troop movements appears to be accurate," the colonel said, turning toward Riley. "We believe they're preparing for a major counter-offensive, and we've begun moving troops accordingly."

Riley nodded, happy that the colonel was acting on her information, but she knew there was more she could do to help the allied forces.

"I'd like to stay on in an advisory role, if I may," she said. "I have more knowledge about German and Russian troop movements that you might find valuable."

The colonel glanced in the direction of the officer on the sofa and paused.

"We've got a more important operation you can help us with," he said. "Do you speak German, by any chance?"

"Genug um durchzukommen," Riley nodded, widening her eyes in surprise at her sudden ability to speak another language. Somehow, the time machine had the ability to transport her to another era and simultaneously give her the skills to adapt to her new surroundings.

"Good," the colonel said, swinging his arm in the direction of the other officer. "This is Major Jamieson. He's in charge of a special operation that we'd like to enlist both of your services for. I'll let him brief you on the particulars. Major?"

The officer stood up and walked over to a large map of Europe hanging on the colonel's wall.

"Our surveillance planes have noticed some suspicious activity near the Bavarian Alps," the major said, pointing to an area in southern Germany. "The Germans are constructing a fortified building in the Black Forest with a considerable amount of heavy machinery moving in and out. We have no idea what they're up to, but if it's some kind of new weapon, we'd rather find out before our troops move onto German soil."

"What do you want us to do?" Riley said, glancing at the captain with a confused expression.

"You've proven to have a special talent for gathering enemy intel," the colonel said. "We want you to get close to the top general in the southern command and find out what they're up to."

Riley paused for a moment, peering at the colonel and the major with a wrinkled forehead.

"How exactly do you expect me to do that?"

"You've shown yourself to be very resourceful so far," the colonel smiled, glancing at the captain. "You seem to have a knack for slipping behind enemy lines and disarming whomever you come into contact with."

"So you want me to *sleep* with this general?" Riley said, remembering his earlier comment about her getting into the commander's pants.

"Not necessarily," the colonel said. "We just want you to get close enough to him and gain enough of his confidence to learn about their plans."

"How will he not suspect I'm a spy?" Riley said, wondering what the hell she'd gotten herself into this time.

"We're going to construct an elaborate cover for you," the major said, resting on the edge of the colonel's desk. "We have German-speaking operatives on the other side who can make a suitable introduction, and we'll supply you with listening devices to bug the general's office."

"How do you want me to assist in this operation?" Captain Miller said, suddenly concerned for Riley's safety.

"You're going to be our commander on the ground," the major said. "You'll direct the operation from a safe distance and liaise with this office to keep us abreast of progress. In the event we need to take action against the fortress, you'll be our point man for leading the attack."

"How are you going to slip us into the country undetected?" the captain said.

"We'll fly you and your team to Switzerland, then our German operative will drive you over the border and set you up in a safe house. You'll be able to monitor communications from there and provide logistical support as necessary."

Riley shifted uncomfortably on her chair.

"While I work alone in the middle of the hornet's nest?" she said.

"In a manner of speaking," the major said. "But you'll be disguised as one of the enemy, and your German handler will be standing by to extricate you if things get out of control."

"Do you trust this handler?" Riley said, still not sure she was ready to sign up for such a dangerous mission.

"She's a young woman, not much older than you," the major said. "Unbeknownst to the High Command, she's one quarter Jewish, so she has plenty of reasons to hate the Germans and keep her identity secret. Plus, she already has an administrative position at their Munich headquarters, so she can keep a close eye on you."

Riley paused for a long moment, darting her eyes between the major and the colonel, then she turned her head to glance at the captain, who was sitting quietly by her side. He peered back at her and tilted his head, as if to suggest the plan might work.

"Are you willing to help us?" the colonel said. "We can't force you to do this, but you've already put yourself in the line of fire and proven your intelligence-gathering skills. We could use someone with your capabilities."

Riley looked up at the map of Europe on the wall, knowing how quickly the political landscape was about to change and exactly what was at stake. She turned back toward the major and the colonel, and nodded.

"I don't know what the hell *else* I'm going to do while I'm stuck here," she said. "Let's get this operation started."

6

———

Later that afternoon, the major briefed Riley and the captain and a group of hand-picked intelligence agents on the operation. Operating under the alias Greta Schrader, Riley's cover was that she'd recently graduated from the Munich Polytechnical University and was looking for gainful employment to support the German war machine. Her father had been killed in battle, and she was living alone with her grandmother on his small military pension in Stuttgart.

Her German handler would make the necessary introductions at the Munich Southern Command and help her plant the listening devices. The captain and his team would work offsite monitoring communications, passing along necessary intel to the major's office using the latest encryption equipment. If Riley's cover were blown, the captain and his team would be responsible for extracting her to safety, using the German handler as an intermediary.

After the exhausting two-hour briefing, Riley and the captain retired to the mess hall for a much-needed dinner.

"Are you sure you're up for this?" he said, peering at

Riley across their narrow lunchroom table.

"I've been in scarier situations than this and managed to come out the other side," Riley nodded, reflecting back on her two previous time travel adventures. "I just hope my German speaking skills are up to the job. The last thing I need is to be exposed by a top SS general."

"Just how far are you willing to go?" the captain said, chewing his food slowly.

"You mean am I willing to sleep with the general if it comes down to it, to gain his confidence?"

"If it comes to that."

"Your job is to make sure it *doesn't* come to that," Riley smiled. "With all these technical specialists assigned to our team, the listening devices should do the lion's share of the intelligence gathering, right?"

"Right," the captain nodded.

"Besides," Riley said, reaching over the table to place her hand over his. "I've got *you* to give me all the intimate contact I need."

"I think we should keep an arms-length distance in our endeavors from this point forward," the captain said, pulling his hand away. "Besides the fact that it will distract our focus, we can't afford to let anyone know there's anything more than a professional relationship between us. I mean, I'm technically your boss now."

"I haven't been officially inducted into the Army, the last time I checked," Riley huffed. "I'm *volunteering* for this operation, remember?"

"Yes, but I'm in charge of coordinating it."

"Well, you can coordinate it all you want, but I'm going to be the one in the lion's den. Everything hinges on my ability to gather the intel from the inside. The way I see it, it's more like you're working for *me*."

"Let's not split hairs over it," the captain said. "We're a team, that's all that matters. We'll all be working together to ensure the success of the mission and to watch your back."

"Well, I hope it's not just my *back* you'll be watching," Riley grinned. "I hope you'll be thinking of certain other body parts on lonely nights, like you were when you were lying next to me in the room next door."

"It'll be hard not to," the captain sighed, glancing out of the corner of his eyes to make sure no one was within earshot.

"Can I call you Jim then, now that we know each other a little better?" Riley smiled.

"In private, yes," the captain said. "But when we're working with the rest of the group, it's probably best you address me by my proper rank."

"Yes, captain," Riley said, lifting her hand up to her temple in mock salute. "Whatever you say, boss."

The following morning, the commando team changed into civilian clothes and clamored into a lorry to the Bastogne airport, where the major was waiting on the tarmac next to a cargo plane. He greeted Riley when she got off the truck, handing her a manila envelope.

"These are your cover papers," he said. "Your German passport, identity papers, resume, and graduation certificate. Your local contact will look after everything else that you need. She'll meet you in Davos and arrange for your transportation to Munich. If you have any other personal effects on your person, now's the time to ditch them. It's better not to have any other documents floating around Germany that can tie you back to the States."

"I arrived here pretty empty-handed," Riley nodded, not willing to disclose the one American artifact she wasn't willing to give up. Strapped to the inside of her ankle stocking was her slim time machine. It was the one safety net she knew that could get her out of any jam whenever she needed it.

"Alright," the major said. "I'll leave you in the capable hands of Captain Miller. You two know your orders. We'll be looking forward to receiving your progress reports."

"Yes, sir," Riley nodded, strolling toward the rear of the cargo plane as its propellers coughed into action.

During the long flight to Switzerland, the team sat quietly facing one another on opposite sides of the empty cargo bay, contemplating the upcoming mission. Everyone knew it was dangerous, none more so than Riley. As the plane jostled and bounced through the turbulent air, she sat stoically beside Captain Miller, feeling his muscular thigh flapping against hers, wishing she could reach out and hold his hand. He was the one connection she trusted to keep her safe, and she missed his firm embrace and soft caress.

When the plane landed three hours later and the cargo door opened, an attractive dark-haired woman was waiting for them on the tarmac.

"Captain Miller?" she said, shaking the captain's hand. "My name's Petra, and I'll be looking after you the rest of the way."

"Yes," the captain said. "I recognize you from the dossier. This is Riley, our inside asset."

Jim turned toward Riley, and the two women shook hands.

"Let's get everyone away from prying eyes," Petra said. "The less we're seen together, the better. The Germans have eyes everywhere."

Petra led the group to a commercial truck parked at the side of the airport, then she lifted the canvas flap covering the rear cargo area, directing the team to climb in.

"Propane tanks?" Jim said, peering at the large metal canisters covering the floorboards.

"Fuel for German industry," Petra nodded. "One of the few useful exports that Switzerland can provide as a neutral country. There's a false bottom under the floorboards, but you and your team can sit next to the canisters until we get to the border. I'll sit up front with Riley to prepare her for the next phase of the mission."

"Okay," Jim hesitated, wary about sitting next to the highly flammable tanks for the next fifty kilometers.

"Just don't light up any cigarettes back here," Riley grinned. "We don't want you blowing yourself up before we get into enemy territory."

Petra climbed in the driver's seat and Riley opened the front passenger door, sitting next to her on the padded bench seat.

While Petra cranked up the diesel engine and put the truck into gear, she turned to Riley and smiled.

"So, how did you manage to get yourself roped into the clandestine affair?" she said.

"I kind of fell into it," Riley said, not willing to tell her too much information about her previous life just yet. "The commanding officer of the front line saw that I had a gift for intelligence gathering and thought that he could put my German language skills to good use.

"Dann sprichst du deutsch?" Petra said.

"Ja," Riley said. "Obwohl es noch nicht getestet wurde."

For the rest of the trip, the two women spoke German so Petra could test her fluency and let Riley practice up.

"You speak German pretty well for an American," Petra said. "Where did you learn it?"

"At university," Riley lied, knowing Petra would never believe her story about how the time machine had landed her here.

"You barely look old enough to be in university," Petra said, peering over at her.

"I could say the same of you," Riley smiled. "You seem far too young to be tangled up in all this espionage business."

"I'm twenty-three, although everyone says I look much younger. We'll have to give you a different haircut, more befitting of your role. As a recent university grad, you'll need to look closer to my age."

Riley turned her head to glance at the pretty double-agent out of the corner of her eyes. She had long eyelashes and bright doe eyes, framed by high cheekbones and a thick, sensuous lips. As the truck jostled over the bumpy local road, her full breasts bounced in her loose-fitting cotton t-shirt, and Riley felt her panties moistening again, remembering her recent lesbian affair during her last adventure in the U.S. Wild West.

"Well, if it'll make me look half as good as you, I'm game," she said. "I suppose part of my cover is to look irresistible, after all."

Petra turned her face to peer at the young schoolgirl for a long moment, then she smiled.

"I don't think you have much to worry about," she said. "Something tells me you'll be distracting the attention of the top brass in no time."

7

—————

When their truck neared the Austrian border, Petra got out and pulled open the hidden hatch for the concealed compartment under the floorboards, where Jim and the rest of the crew piled into the narrow space, lying face-up.

"It's not very roomy," Petra said before closing the hatch. "But it's the only way to keep you hidden from the border inspectors."

"What if they discover the hidden compartment?" Jim said. "We'll be trapped in here like sitting ducks with no way to defend ourselves."

"The sideboards have a release mechanism on the inside," Petra nodded. "If I give you the signal, you can kick them out and roll out to the sides."

"What will be your signal?"

"You'll hear my pistol firing," Petra said. "That means you've only got seconds to escape. Keep your wits about you and listen to the conversation at the border. If the guards ask me to get out of the truck, be prepared to act."

"Great," Jim said. "We'll be packed like sardines while we wait to see if the enemy opens the lid."

"It's better than being gunned down in the open cargo hold," Petra said.

"Barely," he chuckled, peering nervously at the rest of his crew.

"Don't worry, Jim," Riley smiled. "I've got your back."

"Good to know," he said as Petra closed the compartment.

Fifteen minutes later, the truck rolled up to the border station at the Austrian border. Two German soldiers carrying machine guns approached the sides of the front passenger compartment, asking Petra and Riley for their credentials. They inspected the papers, then the senior officer asked Petra to roll down her window.

"What have you got in the back?" he said, glancing at the covered hatch.

"Propane tanks," Petra said.

"Aren't you girls a little young to be ferrying cargo across the border?"

"All the able-bodied men are on the front lines," Petra smiled. "We're just doing our part for the war effort."

The officer squinted at the women, then he motioned for his comrade to circle around the back.

"Can you get out of the truck, please?" he said.

"Both of us?" Petra said.

"Yes," the border guard said. "It's just protocol."

Riley and Petra stepped out of the cab and followed the two agents to the back of the truck, where the senior officer flipped open the flap. He inspected the canisters, shaking one of them to test its contents, then he knelt down to look under the floorboards, squinting his eyes.

"Why is the floor so thick?" he said suspiciously.

"The propane tanks are heavy," Petra said. "There's extra reinforcement to support their weight."

"Then you won't mind if I fire a few shots in there to make sure you're not carrying anything else?"

"If you don't mind getting blown up by highly flammable fuel," Petra said matter-of-factly.

The officer paused for a moment while he appraised the two women, then he motioned to the other soldier.

"Get a crowbar from the guard shack," he said. "I want to have a look in there before we let them through."

While the other soldier walked toward the shack, Riley glanced at Petra, frozen in fear. Petra peered back at her with a steely gaze, nodding softly. When the second soldier placed his crowbar in the side of the hatch, Petra slowly reached behind her back to retrieve her hidden pistol from her waistband, then she fired it into the officer's temple, dropping him instantly. The other soldier looked up in shock, and without thinking, Riley tackled him to the ground, picking up his dropped crowbar and striking him swiftly in the head with the blunt edge. The rest of the team quickly piled out of the two sides of the underfloor compartment, drawing their pistols.

Jim took one look at the two dead border guards, then peered up at Petra.

"What the hell do we do now?" he said. "How are we going to make it to Germany now that our cover's been blown?"

"There was only two of them," Petra said, looking around to make sure there were no other witnesses. "They didn't have a chance to radio ahead and warn the other command posts. As long as we stay under cover, we should be okay. By the time their bosses figure out what happened here, we should be long gone."

"Okay," Jim said, rubbing his hand along the splintered side and rear hatches. "But I think we'll ride topside the rest of the way. At least we'll have a fighting chance if someone stops us again."

"I suppose the hidden compartment is no good to us now," Petra nodded. "I'll bang the rear window if I see any sign of trouble. You might want to check your weapons just in case."

Jim glanced over at Riley, noticing a drop of blood running down the side of her cheek.

"Are you alright?" he said, pulling her hair back softly. "Have you been hurt?"

"It's just a scratch," Riley said, rubbing her fingers along the side of her head. "I must have cut myself when I tackled the other soldier."

"Let's move their bodies to the ditches," Jim said. "That should buy us a little extra time if other vehicles come through."

After everybody got back in the truck, Petra reached into the glove box and moistened a towel, dabbing it at Riley's temple. The flow of blood soon stopped, and she nodded, satisfied it was only a minor scratch. When she put the truck back into gear, she placed her pistol on the cushion between her legs.

"I don't suppose you've got another one of those?" Riley said. "I'd feel a whole lot better having more than a crowbar to defend myself if we get into trouble again."

"Under your seat, behind the springs," Petra nodded.

Riley reached under her seat and felt a metal object

taped to the springs, and when she pulled it out, she inspected the pistol, turning it around in her hands.

"Do you know how to use it?" Petra said.

"It's a little different from what I'm used to," Riley nodded, testing the weight of it in her hand.

"It's a Walther P38, standard issue for German officers. Just remember to push the safety switch forward next to the hammer and pull the trigger to unlock it before firing."

Riley pointed the pistol toward the footwell and followed Petra's instructions, then she reversed the procedure, resting the gun between her thighs.

"What's the story with you and the captain?" Petra said, peering over at her with a raised eyebrow. "You two seem a little more friendly than most intelligence units."

"You mean his touching my forehead a little earlier?" Riley said, remembering how Jim had asked her to keep their special relationship under wraps. "That wasn't anything. He just wanted to make sure I was alright."

"Whatever you say, sweetheart," Petra smiled, glancing at the gleaming handgun nestled next to her crotch in her tight dungarees.

8

For the next couple of hours, the two women spoke quietly in the front compartment while Petra briefed Riley about the key personnel in the Munich headquarters. Their key contact was the SS Army General Hans Muller, who reported directly to Heinrich Himmler as part of a special operation. All Petra knew was that he was directing construction of a top-secret installation deep in the black forest of Bavaria, hidden away from all but classified eyes. Petra's plan was to get Riley a secretarial position at the Munich office, where the two of them would attempt to plant listening devices while providing cover for each other.

As the truck rolled along the winding highway through the Austrian Alps, Riley peered out her window at the beautiful landscape, forgetting for a moment that they were in the middle of a war zone. But as they approached the German border, Petra suddenly slowed the truck, looking ahead with a worried expression.

"What is it?" Riley said, squinting her eyes in the direction of the border post.

"Something's not right," Petra said, lowering her hand toward her pistol. "There's too many guards for such a small border station. Normally, there's only two or three soldiers manning the post."

Riley glanced down the road, noticing a large group of armed soldiers massing in front of the gate, with one of the soldiers holding up his hand as he walked toward the truck, pointing his automatic machine gun in their direction.

"They must have heard about the disturbance at the other border crossing," Petra said, placing her pistol on top of her thigh.

She rapped her knuckle on the window to the rear compartment, sliding it open slowly.

"We've got some trouble up ahead," she said, keeping her vision focused on the group a hundred yards down the road. "We're going to have to bail out. When I give the signal, I want you to tumble out the back and drop a loaded grenade in the cargo hold."

"What about the two of you?" Jim said, nodding at his crew as he unfastened a grenade from his belt.

"We'll wait a few moments longer, then jump out the side doors. With any luck, we can time it so the truck explodes before the Germans have time to react."

"With any luck?" Riley said, snapping her head in Petra's direction.

"Just hold onto your firearm and roll when we hit the ground," Petra said, slowing the truck a little further. "We'll need to get as far away from the truck as possible before the grenade explodes. This thing is going to light up like the Fourth of July when it ignites. Get ready..."

Petra placed her left hand over her door latch and nodded toward Riley.

"Now!" she shouted to the men in the back. Jim pulled

the pin on his grenade, then he and the rest of his crew jumped out the back of the moving truck.

"One, two, three..." Petra counted calmly, then she swung open her door, nodding toward Riley as she dropped onto the pavement, rolling toward the side ditch.

When the crossing guards saw what was happening, they opened fire at the two women, but it was too late. Within seconds, a giant explosion rocked the front of the guard shack, sending the soldiers flying in every direction. When the smoke cleared, Petra pulled herself out of the ditch, making sure there was no more movement in the direction of the shack, then she wandered onto the road, watching Riley and the rest of the crew walking slowly toward her.

"Is everybody okay?" she said.

"Just a few bruises," Jim nodded, surveying the rest of his crew. "How about you, Riley?"

"Only my pride's hurt," she said, peering at Petra with bulging eyes. "I didn't realize we were riding an improvised bomb."

"You're soon going to learn that it's best to have a back-up plan for *everything*," Petra said, glancing at the blazing border station.

"What now?" Jim said. "How are we going to get the rest of the way to Munich?"

"We're going to have to *walk* the rest of the way," Petra said. "But it's best we split up into small groups. We'll be less conspicuous that way. It should take us three or four hours to get to the safe house on foot. Stay off the road and watch out for German patrols. We'll meet up again later tonight."

"What if one of us gets captured?" one of the agents said.

"Don't," Petra said. "The Germans will torture you,

compromising our entire operation. You'd be better off killing yourself than falling into the hands of the Gestapo."

"Can I go with you?" Riley said, suddenly feeling her heart pounding in her chest.

"Yes," Petra nodded, looking at her watch. "The rest of you split up into teams of two and meet up at the safe house at twenty-two hundred."

Riley peered toward Jim and he locked eyes with her, nodding silently. Even though he was ostensibly the leader of the group, they both knew Petra was their best chance of making it to safety.

9

———

Later that evening, the group reassembled at the safe house in downtown Munich, where Jim briefed the team on the next steps for the mission.

"The first step in our intelligence gathering is planting listening devices in General Muller's office so we can tap into his conversations," he said. "I'm going to let our lead tech specialist, Benjamin Martinez, give Riley and Petra an overview of how they work and where to plant them. Then we'll talk about the second phase of intel gathering, and finally what our backup plan will be if anyone's cover is blown."

Jim motioned to his associate then took a seat.

"Ben, do you want to take it from here?"

Ben reached into a leather case and pulled out some small electronic devices that looked like little ladybugs.

"These devices are small radio transmitters with a multi-directional microphone," he said, handing one to each of the girls. "You'll want to position them as close to the general's desk as possible, but not in such an obvious place that he or one of his staff might find them. So not directly on his desk, or any place he can easily check."

"What about inside his telephone?" Riley said, thinking that would be the easiest way to pick up his conversations.

"Too obvious," Ben said. "His staff will be regularly sweeping the place, and that's one of the first places they'll check."

"How about behind a painting on his wall?" Petra said, having some knowledge of the general's office layout from occasional glimpses through his open door.

"Same thing," Ben said. "Too easy to check, and too easy to find. It needs to be someplace hidden that he and his staff would be unlikely to check. Can you describe the layout of his office?"

"It's a typical office," Petra nodded. "There's a big desk next to the window overlooking the courtyard, some books in a case on one wall, maps and a painting of the Fuhrer on the other walls, and two small chairs facing the desk."

"What kind of chairs?"

"They look to be upholstered in leather, with wooden arms, in the Chippendale style–"

"Those might work," Ben said. "The upholstery will likely be pinned to the underside of the frame with a thin mesh covering on the bottom surface. If you could slip one of the bugs under the mesh and refasten the leather, that would provide a clear signal and be fairly unobtrusive."

"Shouldn't we try to plant more than one?" Riley said. "In case the other is found or doesn't work properly?"

"Actually, the fewer the better," Ben said. "The more we plant, the more likely they are to be found. If you can successfully plant one, we'll test the signal from here and as long as it transmits, we'll start with that."

"How will we smuggle them into the headquarters?"

Petra said. "The Gestapo chief sweeps the office regularly, looking for suspicious equipment and documents. The last thing we need is for him to find one of these bugs on our person."

"We can make a modification to the heel of your shoes," Ben nodded. "We'll carve a small hole inside the block, where we'll place the bug. You'll just need to pry it off with a sturdy nail file when the time is right, then press down hard to reconnect the attachment nails."

"Okay," Riley said, turning her head to look at Petra while they nodded toward each other. "What's the next phase in the plan?"

"That one will be a little more difficult," Jim said, rising up from his sitting position at the side of his desk. "Once we get an idea as to what they're using the fortress for, we'll want to get our hands on documents and blueprints of the installation. These are likely to be kept in his safe, which will have a secret combination."

"How do you expect us to find that?" Petra said.

"With a hidden camera," Ben said, pulling another device out of his case. "But this one needs direct line of sight, so it will be harder to conceal. Do you know where he keeps his safe?"

"It's on the wall next to the window behind his desk," Petra nodded. "But I've never seen him open it with his door ajar, and I have no idea where we'd plant the camera to get a clear line of sight."

"It's better if we plant it slightly off to the side, since he'll likely be blocking the tumblers with his body when he opens the safe. How close is the bookcase?"

"Maybe ten feet or so away..."

"If we provide you with a small personal camera, do you think you'd be able to take a picture of it sometime? That way, we could reproduce one of the books and plant the camera in the binding. All you'd have to do is replace it in a moment of distraction."

"A moment of distraction?" Petra said.

"An emergency of some kind, maybe an air-raid siren or some such thing."

"Our army is a long way from entering this part of Germany," Riley said, reflecting back on her knowledge of allied troop positions. "Can you manufacture one if need be?"

"Possibly," Jim nodded. "This mission has been given top priority at the highest levels. Of course, if you can provide a *different* kind of distraction, that will save us a lot of trouble. That's why we're positioning two of you at their headquarters. If one of you can divert the general's attention long enough, the other one could plant the device..."

"How do you propose we do that?" Riley said.

"Once you determine his routine, it might not be as difficult as it sounds."

"And how will we conceal our cameras from the Gestapo?" Petra said.

Ben reached into his bag and handed each of the women a small lipstick tube.

"These tubes have a pinhole camera under the sticker on the bottom. Once you remove the sticker and turn the tube one entire cycle clockwise, the shutter will open and take a picture. All you have to do is aim it in the direction of the bookcase."

"Very ingenious," Petra said, twisting the tube until she heard a small click.

"What's the backup plan if one of us gets caught?" Riley said.

"It's best you minimize trips back to the safe house once

you're both comfortably installed at the headquarters," Jim said. "It will invite too much suspicion and lead the Gestapo back to us. We'll communicate via letter drops at a designated location. If we uncover any suspicion as to your real identities, we'll notify you with a red mark on the envelope."

"What if there isn't time to notify each other that way?"

"We'll plant an explosive device near the front door. If you hear it go off, that means you've only got a few seconds to make your escape. Then we'll reconvene at another location to plan next steps."

"Where will I stay in the meantime?" Riley said.

"Petra has a small apartment on the Blumenstrasse. You two will hole up there while we monitor communications from this side and provide logistical support as required."

"Sounds like you've thought of everything," Riley nodded, starting to feel more comfortable.

"Not everything," Petra said. "There's always something that interferes with the best-laid plans. Especially when the Gestapo are constantly fishing around..."

10

After the intelligence briefing finished, Riley and Petra took a streetcar back to Petra's apartment, where the two women shared a late-night snack before turning in for the night.

"This goulash is just what I needed after a long and stressful day," Riley nodded over Petra's small kitchen table. "I could eat a horse after going the whole day without food."

"It's the best I could scare up on short notice," Petra said. "It's got a little bit of everything. Chunks of beef, carrots, potatoes, onion, bell peppers..."

"It's delicious," Riley said, gobbling down the hearty broth. "Maybe I can cook the next meal..."

"I'll pick up some extra provisions at the market when I return from the headquarters," Petra nodded. "It's best that you don't venture out on your own while I'm away, since you don't know the lay of the land. You don't want to arouse any unnecessary suspicion with so many German agents crawling around.

"What's your plan for inserting me into the headquarters?" Riley said.

"I'll pass along your resume to the office manager. They're always looking for new secretaries with so many women losing their husbands in the war. Someone's got to look after the little ones at home."

"Maybe my young age and unmarried status will work to my advantage then," Riley smiled.

"I suspect it will," Petra nodded. "After the Gestapo chief vets your background, they'll likely call you in for an interview. Can you type?"

"Over a hundred words per minute," Riley nodded, not yet ready to divulge her laptop use as part of her studies at MIT.

"You seem to tick all the boxes," Petra nodded. "The fact that you're so pretty will likely put a lock on it. These high-ranking officers at the headquarters are a randy lot. You'll probably have to fight off their affections at one point or another."

"What about you?" Riley said, peering over her spoon at Petra's long eyelashes. "How do you manage to keep them at bay? Or is that part of the undercover job, to get into their pants to gain their confidence?"

"Not if I can help it," Petra frowned. "I despise Nazis. There'd have to be an awfully compelling reason for me to go that far to sacrifice my personal dignity. Besides, I don't really swing that way."

"Oh?" Riley said, feeling her pussy fluttering at the suggestion she preferred women. "What made you volunteer for this operation in the first place?"

"You probably noticed on my dossier that I'm one quarter Jewish. I've managed to disguise it so far, but my grandfather was apprehended as part of Himmler's final solution. I have no idea where he's been taken and I fear the worst. The sooner we can defeat the Germans, the more lives we'll be able to save."

"I'm sorry to hear that," Riley nodded, feeling a stronger connection to the pretty German with each passing moment. "How did you manage to hide your connection to him?"

"I've had an elaborate cover constructed by inside agents, just like you."

"I guess we're both going to be canaries in the coal mine, then," Riley chuckled.

"Canaries in the what...?" Petra said, pinching her eyebrows together.

"It's an English expression," Riley said. "It means if there's ever a gas leak in the mine, the canary will be the first to succumb, so the rest of the miners will have time to get out alive."

"Let's hope there isn't a leak in our little underground operation then," Petra said with a lopsided grin. "Because if there is, we'll be the first ones to be sacrificed."

After Riley helped Petra clean the dishes, she peered around the small apartment, wondering where she would sleep.

"Where do you want me to rest tonight?" she said.

"There should be enough room on the sofa," Petra said, pointing toward the small couch in her living room. "But if you find it uncomfortable, you're welcome to sleep with me. There's enough room on my double bed for two."

The girls performed their nightly ablutions in the restroom, then Petra kissed Riley softly on the cheek and bade her good night, with Riley tucking herself under a blanket on the sofa and Petra heading into her room. When Riley lay her head down on the armrest, she peered through the open crack in Petra's door, noticing her changing out of her clothes as she undressed beside her bedside lamp. The glow from the lamp cast just enough light on her naked body for Riley to peer at her firm, pointed breasts and tight round ass. After tossing and turning on the lumpy sofa for a few minutes while becoming increasingly aroused thinking about Petra's sexy body, she pulled the blanket around her naked body and walked toward Petra's room, edging the door open gently.

"I think I'll take you up on your offer to share your bed, after all," she smiled.

"I was hoping you'd feel that way," Petra said, flipping the bed sheet down. "But I don't think you'll need the extra blanket. It's plenty warm enough in here already."

11

———————

The following morning, Petra left to resume her administrative job at the Munich headquarters while Riley reviewed her intelligence dossier. Little was known about the SS general other than he had a decorated military background and was hand-picked by Himmler to oversee the secret fortress operation. He looked handsome and distinguished, somewhere in his mid-fifties, and Riley squinted her eyes, wondering how he could get so wrapped up in Hitler's world domination scheme.

But her mind kept drifting back to Petra and their passionate lovemaking the previous night. It had been a while since she'd felt the soft skin of a woman next to her, and as attracted as she was to Jim, it was a thrill to tangle their bodies together and climax in each other's arms. As she thought about their pussies rubbing together under the warm covers, her hand drifted between her legs, rubbing her button under the front of her pants. When Petra suddenly swung the door of the apartment open, Riley slid her hand out of her pants, returning her attention to the dossier.

"Find anything interesting in there?" Petra said, dropping a bag of groceries on the table.

"Nothing more than we already knew," Riley said, feeling her heart fluttering at the sight of her pretty German associate. "General Muller actually looks quite handsome. It's a pity we'll be putting a kibosh on his plans–"

"Don't let his pretty blue eyes distract you," Petra said, beginning to put the food in the cupboards. "He's as evil as they come. Among other things, the SS commands the network of concentration camps where the Jews are put to death. He can be quite charming, but you mustn't forget what he's trying to do. Which is nothing less than the subjugation of the free world according to Hitler's grand plan."

"Don't worry," Riley said, reaching out to hold Petra's hand. "I haven't forgotten our mission. Besides, I only have eyes for you."

"And our handsome *captain*, perhaps?" Petra smiled, pulling a long cucumber out of the grocery bag and rubbing it gently against the side of Riley's cheek.

"He has his charms to be sure," Riley said, stroking the shaft of the cucumber slowly. "But it looks like I'll be assigned to you for the remainder of the mission. I'm just going to have to make the best of a difficult situation."

"Well, it's about to get more complicated," Petra said, resting the cucumber on the table. "The Gestapo chief has approved your credentials and the office manager wants you to come in for an interview tomorrow morning."

"Already?" Riley said.

"The Germans are efficient about everything," Petra nodded. "They have a procedure for everything, and they don't mess around when they set their sights on something."

"Speaking of messing around," Riley said, picking up the cucumber and nibbling on the end of it with the tips of her teeth. "I've been thinking about you all day long, and I've been dying to climb back into bed with you. How'd you like to take a little break before we start to prepare dinner?"

"You're twisting my arm, girl," Petra smiled, grabbing the cucumber and flexing it softly in her hands. "Why don't we take a little bit of dinner with us to the bedroom?"

Riley peered at Petra with a devilish grin, then the two women skipped toward the bed, tearing off their clothes and giggling excitedly while the cucumber flopped beside their bodies. Petra raised up on her knees and picked up the tuber, holding it in front of her bare pussy, mimicking the movement of a man's penis.

"Are you *sure* you're not missing Captain Miller?" she teased.

Riley leaned forward and engulfed the end of the cucumber in her mouth, wrapping her tongue around the edges.

"Maybe just a little," she smiled. "But perhaps we can have the best of both worlds."

She pulled the moistened end of the cucumber toward her pussy and inserted it into her hole, then she lay down, spreading her legs apart, inviting Petra to do the same with the other end.

She glanced at Riley's dripping pussy with the gourd sticking out of her like a fat dildo, then she lay down with her hips facing Riley, pointing the other end toward her slit. When they shifted their hips together, the cucumber sank deeper into their pussies while they groaned in unison.

"Mmm," Petra hummed. "Maybe there's something to be said for having a good old *fucking* once in a while, after all."

"It's not quite as warm as a man's cock," Riley nodded. "But it'll do in a pinch. Besides, this way we can fuck each other at the same time. Who needs a man when there's such a juicy substitute standing nearby?"

Petra reached out her hands and Riley intertwined their fingers, pulling their bodies closer together. When the two ends of the improvised dildo sunk all the way into their holes and their vulvas touched, they gasped, rubbing their clits together.

"Holy shit," Petra moaned. "What would Captain Miller say if he could see us now?"

"He probably wouldn't approve," Riley grinned. "You know, wanting to keep up professional appearances and all that..."

"*Fuck* professional appearances," Petra said, turning her body forty-five degrees to rub her ass against the inside of Riley's thigh. "You never know what's going to happen in this crazy war. We don't want to miss any pleasurable moments."

"Speaking of pleasurable moments," Riley panted. "I'm about to have one right now. Hold my hands while I cum against you."

"*Fuck* yes," Petra hissed, throwing her head onto the mattress and arching her back.

"Let it go, babe. I'm going to cum with you."

"Uhnnn!" the two women grunted in delirious climax, gripping each other's hands tightly while they thrashed their bodies together on the bed with the juicy cucumber dripping between their thighs.

12

––––––––––

The next morning, the two women rode a streetcar to the Munich SS headquarters, where Petra introduced Riley to the office manager using her alias. After their brief interview, the Gestapo chief led her to a closed room, where he sat down next to her across a narrow table.

"It says on your identity papers that you were born in Wurzburg," the major said, peering at Riley through narrow eyelids. "You must know the town fairly well then."

"Yes, I suppose so," Riley said, feeling her heart pounding in her chest like a giant drum.

"Then you must be familiar with the famous fresco in the Residenz palace," he nodded. "Do you know who the artist is?"

Riley peered at the Gestapo officer's stark black uniform with its sinister skull-shaped epaulets on the collar, trying to remember all the details she'd reviewed in her thick dossier describing her background as a Bavarian schoolgirl.

"You mean the one on the ceiling of the grand staircase?" she said, trying to remain calm. "That was painted by

Tiepolo, of course. It's purportedly the largest ceiling fresco in the world."

"Um-hmm," the officer nodded with a steely expression. "And your mother died of an overdose after your father was killed on duty. Isn't that somewhat convenient?"

"I'd hardly call it *convenient*," Riley said. "My grandmother and I have had to live on his small pension ever since then. It hasn't been easy–"

"What about your grand*father*?" the major said, testing Riley's nerves to see if he could expose any irregularities in her story. "Why isn't he living with you too?"

"He died of a heart attack many years ago," Riley said, feeling the palms of her hands begin to sweat.

"That must have been quite traumatic for you, losing so many of your family members while you were so young."

"Yes," Riley said, forcing tears into her eyes while she played her role to the fullest.

"We'll need to speak with your grandmother to verify these details," the major said nonchalantly.

"Of course," Riley nodded, praying that the agent her team had planted in Wurzburg as her grandmother would hold up just as well as she had under intense questioning.

"Alright then," the major said, suddenly standing up and striking his heels together, thrusting his right hand forward over his shoulder. "Heil Hitler!"

"Heil Hitler," Riley said, standing up and trying her best to mimic the colonel's gesture with an equal measure of conviction.

A few minutes later, the handsome general that Riley had seen in her dossier emerged from his office, walking toward her desk in the anteroom and holding out his hand.

"I understand you're our new secretary," he said, smiling at Riley. "Do you have a few minutes to chat with me in my office? I like to become familiar with my new staff before beginning to work together."

"Of course," Riley said, feeling the muscles in her legs beginning to shake under her desk. "May I take a moment to freshen up first in the ladies' room?"

"Of course," the general said. "I'll be waiting in my office."

Riley rose from her desk, and as she turned in the direction of the washroom, she caught a glimpse of Petra as she peered out of the corner of her eye. She nodded softly, offering Riley silent encouragement.

Knowing she was about to enter the general's office for the first time, Riley closed herself into one of the cubicles, fishing her metal nail file out of her purse. Then she raised her right foot, prying off the heel of her shoe to fetch the small bug that Ben had concealed under her sole. After placing it in the side pocket of her dress, she reattached the heel to the base of her shoe, then she straightened her hair and wiped the sheen of perspiration from her brow.

When she presented herself in front of the general's open door, he motioned for her to come inside, asking her to close the door behind her.

"Please, have a seat," he said, standing up and extending his hand toward one of the guest chairs facing his desk.

Just as Petra had described in their earlier intelligence briefing, it was a leather armchair with curved wooden handles and clawfoot legs. Riley could feel her arms quivering as she faced the imposing general, and she clasped her hands gently on her lap to still her nerves.

"You're a recent graduate of Munich Polytechnical, I see," the General nodded, reviewing Riley's resume behind his desk.

"Yes," Riley said, trying to control her shaking voice.

"That might come in handy, given the nature of our operations here in Southern Germany."

"Any way I can help the cause," Riley nodded, letting her right hand slowly drift down to her side.

"You're not bitter about losing your parents to the war effort?" the general said.

Riley could feel the row of flat thumbtacks holding the leather seat covering to the underside of the chair, and she smiled, happy that from his vantage point ten feet away behind his large desk that his line of sight didn't extend below her shoulders.

"Not bitter," she said, wedging the nail of her thumb under one of the tacks, trying to pry it loose. "Only sad and more determined than ever to prevail over our enemies."

The general paused as his eyes darted over Riley's face, glancing down at her cleavage, partly exposed in her tightly buttoned dress.

"You seem to look awfully young for someone to have already graduated from university. Are you sure you're up for the rigors of this office? Things can get pretty hectic in here from time to time."

"Just good genes, I guess," Riley nodded, feeling the tack separate from the wood and drop into her palm. "As for the demands of the office, if I can survive the rigors of technical college, I imagine I can handle just about anything."

"Yes," the general said. "That was *also* a very male-dominated culture. I understand that less than five percent of the graduating class was comprised of women. How did you find working alongside so many leering classmates while you tried to complete your studies?"

"I just focused on the task at hand," Riley said, raising her hand to slip the tack into her side pocket while sliding the listening device into her palm. Then she edged her hand back down over the side of the chair, slipping the bug into the gap under the thin fabric, swallowing hard while the general peered into her eyes.

"I've found that if you show any vulnerabilities among men, they'll just take advantage of you."

"That's a wise credo," the general said. "I think you'll fit right in around here. Our office manager Wilma will get you set up with the protocol of our headquarters. In the meantime, feel free to see me if you have any questions."

The general stood up from behind his desk and walked around to face Riley, extending his hand to her once again.

"Welcome to our team, Greta," he said.

"Thank you, sir," Riley said, placing her sweaty palm in his grip.

She hadn't had enough time to reinsert the tack under the chair and now it was too late. She'd just have to hope that no one noticed the missing piece until she had a chance to replace it during another visit to his office. For now, the bug would have to stay partially exposed until she had a chance to patch it up.

As she turned to exit the office, the general suddenly called out to her.

"Aren't you forgetting something?" he said.

Riley turned around to face him, suddenly feeling weak in the knees, fearing he'd noticed her planting the listening device under the chair.

"Sir?" she squeaked.

"Heil Hitler!" the general said, clamping his boots together and raising his hand in salute.

"Heil Hitler," Riley said, barely able to raise her shaking arm.

13

———

When Petra and Riley returned home later that night, they found an envelope hidden in the newsstand near their apartment. When they closed the door, they opened the letter while Riley read the inscription.

Bug planted successfully. Monitoring conversations. Talking about a uranium enrichment facility. Our intelligence experts say it's for a big bomb. Standby for further instructions.

"A bomb?" Petra said, peering at Riley with a quizzical look. "What kind of bomb?"

"I've heard of this type of bomb," Riley nodded, her face suddenly turning pale. "It's a nuclear device with the capability to wipe out an entire city with a single explosion."

What?" Petra said. "How is that even possible?"

"It's a physics thing," Riley said. "Something to do with splitting the atom. If you can do it with the right material, it releases a tremendous amount of energy. I had no idea the Germans were that close to developing such a weapon."

"So what do we do now?" Petra said, peering at Riley with a worried expression.

"We're going to have to speed up our plans," Riley said. "If the Nazis complete construction of a nuclear bomb, it can completely turn the tide of the war. Besides wiping out hundreds of thousands of troops, if they were to drop it on London or Moscow, it could break the resolve of the alliance."

"How do you know so much about this bomb?" Petra said, shaking her head.

"I studied some physics at college in the States," Riley said, still not ready to tell Petra that she'd come from the future. "It's got something to do with Einstein's theory of relativity."

"*Albert* Einstein?" Petra said. "The famous physicist who fled Germany when Hitler rose to power?"

"Yes, but there are many other German scientists with advanced knowledge of nuclear physics. This is apparently the nerve center of the operation."

Petra picked up the letter from Jim and peered over its contents.

"Captain Miller said to standby, awaiting further instructions."

"I don't think we should wait," Riley nodded. "We have no idea how far advanced their development program is. We need to get our hands on the plans for that fortress as soon as possible and identify the scientists involved in its operation. They're almost as valuable as the bomb itself. We can't afford to let them fall into Russian hands."

"Russian hands?" Petra said. "Aren't they our *allies*?"

"Maybe now, but they're no friend of the west. Stalin will be just as bad as Hitler when it comes to seizing territory. We can't destroy the fortress only to have the technology fall into the hands of another world power."

"There's something that you haven't been telling me,"

Petra said, placing her hand over Riley's. "You know things nobody else could possibly know. Where are you really from, and how did you get mixed up in this operation?"

Riley paused for a long moment, contemplating whether she should tell Petra how she really landed here.

"I'm not sure you'd believe me if I told you the truth," she said.

"You've already shown that you have special powers," Petra smiled, gripping Riley's hand. "How much more fantastic can it get?"

"You have no idea," Riley smiled, letting out a deep sigh.

T he two women retired to the bedroom, where they sat cross-legged on the mattress while Riley told Petra about her mysterious time machine and the places she'd traveled. When she finished, Petra stared back at her with her mouth agape.

"I told you it was an unbelievable story," Riley said.

"I believe you," Petra said. "How else could you have all this knowledge of advance troop movements and secret operations?"

Riley tilted her head and shrugged her shoulders.

"Well, it's not much help when the major powers are the ones pulling the strings that determine the course of the war."

"Can't you travel further back in time and eliminate Hitler before he rises to power, or at least warn the Americans and British about his plans?"

"It's not as easy as that," Riley said. "I can't set it to take me exactly where and when I want. It's kind of a random thing, taking me to unexpected places. Besides, nobody else would believe me if I told them I was a time traveler from the future."

"They would if you showed them your time travel device. Where is it now?"

"It's in a safe place," Riley nodded. "But I'm not ready to let anyone else experiment with it. I've seen what happens when powerful people get their hands on powerful technology. For now, it's not much more than a toy that takes me on these crazy adventures."

Petra snuggled up closer to Riley, eager to learn everything she knew.

"What *other* fun toys have they invented in the future?" she said.

"Well, among other things," Riley said, caressing Petra's crotch. "They've invented special cucumbers that vibrate *automatically* to stimulate your private parts."

"You mean like my washing machine?" Petra smiled, wrapping her legs around Riley's hips. "That does wonders to get me off on lonely nights."

"A little," Riley chuckled, pressing her breasts against Petra's. "Just a little more intense and concentrated, a bit like the atomic bomb."

"Well there's nothing we can do about that bomb right now, so why don't we create a little explosion of our own before we go off trying to save the rest of the world?"

"Works for me," Riley said, unclasping Petra's bra and pushing her down on the bed.

14

———

The next morning, General Muller called Riley into his office, asking her to take a seat.

"Do you know how to take shorthand?" he said. "I need to dictate a letter."

"Yes..." Riley said, not sure if her German writing ability was up to her speaking skills.

"Alright then," he said, turning around to peer out his window as he contemplated what he wanted to say.

"Dear Professor Heisenberg," the general dictated.

Heisenberg, Riley thought, pausing her pen. The name sounded familiar, but she couldn't place it.

"I understand that fuel stores are almost complete. I'd like an updated schedule for completion of the weapon..."

Fuel stores? The weapon? Riley thought. Was he talking about the nuclear bomb under development at the fortress? She fished the missing thumb tack out of her side pocket and fumbled underneath the chair, searching for the gap in the fabric. When she found it, she slid the tack back into the hole, pressing it firmly against the leather seam.

"Are you getting all this?" the general said, swinging

around.

"Yes," Riley said, picking up the pen resting on her notepad in her lap.

"I'll need weight and volume dimensions of the device in order to secure delivery to the front," the general continued, turning back around to look out over the courtyard. "Also, the blast radius, so our pilots know the safe distance to drop it..."

Jesus, Riley thought, scribbling furiously on her notepad. *They're getting ready to ship the bomb!*

She peered up, noticing the general lost in thought at the window, and pulled her lipstick camera out of her pocket, tearing off the sticker on the end and aiming it toward the bookcase on the side wall. The general turned around again and squinted his eyes, noticing Riley holding the tube awkwardly next to her lips.

"Am I keeping you from something important?" the general said, stepping toward Riley with renewed interest.

"No," she said, fumbling for an answer. "My lips were just a little dry..."

"I like that color on you," the general said, taking the tube out of her hands and rubbing his finger over the waxy tip. "It's very sexy."

"I'm glad you like it," Riley said, holding her breath as he inspected the tube. Fortunately, he didn't notice the small pinhole on the underside of the tube where the camera lens was hidden.

The general handed the lipstick tube back to her and smiled.

"How'd you like to have dinner with me when we finish up at the office later today?" he said.

Riley paused for a long moment, unsure how to reply. She didn't want to give the general the wrong idea about her intentions, but she recognized it as an opportunity to gain more of his confidence and provide a distraction for their continued espionage efforts at the headquarters.

"Okay," she nodded softly. "Will this dress be appropriate for the event?"

"It'll do just fine," the general smiled, peering down her cleavage. "A tight dress like that is just the thing for what I had in mind."

"Was there anything else you wanted to add to the letter?" Riley said, trying to return the general's attention to the business at hand.

"Oh yes," he said, leaning against the side of his desk as he stared at Riley's curvy legs sticking out below her knee-length dress. "Please advise before end of day. High Command is eager to start the mission. Sincerely, Obergruppen Fuhrer Hans Muller."

After Riley exited General Muller's office, her eyes bulged when she made contact with Petra sitting at her desk. Petra shook her head in puzzlement, then she motioned toward the restrooms, eager to get the dirt on what Riley had uncovered. When they entered the ladies' room, Petra looked under the cubicle doors to make sure they were alone, then she walked up to the vanity mirror, pressing her lipstick tube to her lips.

"What happened in there?" she said to Riley. "You look like you saw a ghost."

"The general asked me to record a letter," Riley said. "They're preparing to ship the bomb. We may only have a few days left."

"*Scheisse*," Petra cursed. "Were you able to replace the

missing tack?"

"Yes, and I managed something else," Riley said, pulling her lipstick tube out of her side pocket and handing it to Petra. "I took a picture of his bookcase. Can you deliver it to Jim sometime tonight? The sooner we're able to uncover the combination to the general's safe, the better. We're going to need the plans to the fortress if we're going to disarm the bomb before they smuggle it out of there."

"Why don't you do it yourself?" Petra smiled, pushing the lipstick back in Riley's direction. "I'm sure he'll be happy to see you again."

"I won't be able to make it tonight," Riley said, putting the stick back in Petra's hand and curling her fingers around it. "The general's asked me out to dinner this evening. I wasn't really in a position to say no."

"How did that happen so suddenly?" Petra said.

"He caught me applying lipstick while I pointed the camera toward his bookcase. I think he took my gesture the wrong way, thinking I was flirting with him or something."

"Does he suspect any foul play?"

"I don't think so," Riley said. "He seemed far more interested in inspecting my cleavage and legs than the hidden camera."

"What if he wants more than just dinner?"

"I might have to humor him," Riley grimaced. "I can't afford to lose his confidence when we're so close to capturing the prize. Besides, it might be an opportunity to distract his attention while you break into his safe."

Petra peered back at Riley in the mirror with a furrowed brow.

"It's going to take something extraordinary to lure him away from his office," she nodded. "If anybody can distract him long enough, it's you."

15

———

Later that evening, General Muller took Riley to one of Munich's fanciest restaurants, seating her at the best table next to a blazing fireplace.

"Good evening, Herr Muller," the maître d' said, bowing when he saw the senior SS officer enter the establishment. "We've reserved your table, if you'll come this way."

The maître d' pulled out one of the chairs for Riley and the general waited until she was seated.

"May I bring you an aperitif to get you started?" the maître d' said.

"Thank you, Klaus," the general nodded. "How about a bottle of your best champagne? I'm in a celebratory mood."

"As you wish, sir," the maître d' said, bowing again before he took his leave.

Riley peered around the restaurant, feeling the heat from the fireplace flame warming her cheeks. The restaurant was packed with German officers wearing the familiar SS uniform, and she could feel her heart pounding in her chest, surrounded by so many enemy soldiers. Just before she returned her attention to the general, she noticed the

Gestapo officer from the office, sitting in a far corner, watching them quietly.

"This is lovely," Riley said, smiling at the general. "Do you always get the best seat at the fanciest restaurants in town?"

"A privilege of my rank, I suppose," the general nodded. "Unless one of my bosses is in town. Everything follows the order of the military hierarchy."

Riley paused, appraising the gilded gold and scarlet insignia emblazoned atop his shoulders and the iron cross hanging between his collar.

"I can't imagine you have many bosses," she said. "You seem to be a pretty important man in this town."

"I've just had the luck to be put in charge of an important operation, that's all," the general said, nodding toward the maître d' when he returned with the champagne. After the waiter uncorked the bottle and filled their glasses, the general raised his glass and smiled.

"Shall we make a toast?" he said. "To great progress and great conquests."

"Heil Hitler," Riley said, unsure how else to respond to the general's gesture.

The general paused after he took a swig of his champagne, running his eyes over her tight dress.

"What brings you to Munich, so far away from your hometown?" he said.

"Just looking for meaningful work, I suppose," Riley nodded. "There's not many engineering jobs in Wurzburg these days."

"Yes," the general nodded. "I suppose most of the technical work has moved to the big factories in the main cities. All our resources seem to be dedicated to the war effort these days."

Riley hesitated for a moment, wondering how she might position herself closer to the general's secret operation.

"I was kind of hoping to put my technical skills to better use than being a secretary," she said, feeling her face becoming redder from the warmth of the fire.

The general peered at her flushed face, captivated by her youthful good looks.

"Do you have any idea what we're working on at the fortress in the mountain?" he said.

"Only an inkling from what you mentioned earlier today," Riley said. "Something about a special weapon..."

"A special weapon indeed," the general nodded. "Something that can change the course of the war and turn our enemies back on their heels."

"I can only imagine–"

"You studied physics as part of your technical studies, did you not?"

"Yes," Riley said.

"Then you know about Einstein's theory of general relativity."

"Every first-year student knows about his famous equation," Riley nodded. "It's the cornerstone of quantum mechanics."

"His theory focused mostly on astronomical phenomena," the general said. "Concerning gravity and the movement of light. But the implications of his research are even more profound at the molecular level."

"How do you mean?" Riley said, feigning ignorance.

"I'm not at liberty to disclose any more details right now," he said. "But it will become apparent to the whole world soon enough."

"It's too bad that it's classified," Riley said, brushing her foot against the general's ankle. "I'd love to see what you're working on."

The general paused again, darting his eyes over Riley's face, trying to divine her intentions.

"I could take you there sometime if you like," he nodded, taking another sip of his champagne. "We'd have to raise your clearance level, of course."

"Do you think Major Hoffmann would be on board with that?" Riley said, glancing in the direction of the Gestapo officer still sitting quietly in the corner.

"He works for me," the general said. "So I'm sure it shouldn't be a problem. I'll talk to him tomorrow and see if I can arrange a tour later in the week."

"That would be wonderful," Riley said, sitting up excitedly in her seat. "Thank you, sir."

"My pleasure," the general said, refilling Riley's champagne glass as he motioned for the maître d' to bring them another bottle.

After dinner, the general walked Riley home through the dusky streets of Munich, pointing out the important government buildings and historical points of interest. The further they walked, the more personal his questions became, prying deeper into her private life.

"You mentioned during your interview that you weren't distracted by the boys at college," he said. "Are you not attracted to men?"

"Of course," Riley said, feeling the hair beginning to raise on her skin, sensing the general's increasing interest in her. "I just never had much interest in the younger ones. They don't have the manners and sophistication of older gentlemen like you."

"So you think I'm *old* then?" the general said, stopping abruptly and turning to look at Riley with a bemused expression.

"No," she said. "I didn't mean it that way. I just meant that you're more worldly and charismatic–"

Suddenly, the general pulled Riley into a nearby alley, pressing her firmly against the brick wall.

"You're an uncommon woman, Greta," he said, lowering his lips toward hers. "Wise beyond your years and extremely beautiful. It's a shame to let all this talent go to waste..."

"Oh general," Riley panted, playing the role of damsel in distress to the hilt. "Take me. I need to feel the touch of a real man..."

The general hiked one side of her dress, then he raised her left knee, pulling her panties below her thighs and reaching between his legs while he unzipped his trousers. When Riley felt his hard erection thrust into her opening, she gasped, feeling the rough stones tearing the back of her dress while he pounded her against the wall. Although she didn't enjoy the impromptu affair, she panted and sighed, putting on her best act of submission. When it was over, the general quickly zipped up his pants, looking around to make sure no one was watching.

"Can you make it home the rest of the way?" he said. "I don't suppose it would be proper for the two of us to be seen in public this way."

"Of course," Riley said, straightening out her dress.

"I'll see you tomorrow, then," the general said. "And please, no word of this to anyone else."

"I wouldn't think of it," Riley said, pulling her purse

under her arm and walking toward the nearest streetcar stop.

When she neared Petra's apartment building, she stopped at the newsstand, finding a new letter from Jim.

Pictures from camera processed, the note said. New camera concealed in book reproduction. Pick up same place tomorrow before going to work. Try to keep general distracted as long as possible. Petra will plant device and will advise re next steps.

As Riley trudged up the steps to Petra's apartment, she shook her head, ashamed at how easily she'd given up her virtue for the cause of the mission.

Maybe I can go back in time and erase this little misjudgment, she thought to herself as she turned the key in Petra's lock. When she opened the door, Petra was sitting at the dining room table, peering back at her with a knowing look.

16

———

The next day, there was a palpable tension at the headquarters as General Muller stayed holed up in his room for most of the morning. Riley wondered if his interest in her had passed now that he'd had his way with her, but shortly before noon, he called her back into his office.

"Greta," he said, closing the door gently behind her. "I wanted to apologize about last night. It was improper of me to force myself on you then to leave you the way I did..."

"It's quite alright, sir," Riley said, standing close to him. "I'm glad you did. I enjoyed our little rendezvous. I only wish it had lasted longer..."

"I was hoping you felt that way," the general said, wrapping his arm around her waist and pulling their bodies together. "I haven't been able to stop thinking about you all day."

Riley could feel his hardening tool pressing against the front of her dress, and as they stumbled toward the side of his office, they bumped up against his bookcase. This time Riley decided to take the initiative, pulling the general's pants down and kneeling in front of him, taking his engorged cock into his mouth. While he groaned and ran his fingers through her hair, she peered up at the bookcase out of the corner of her eyes, locating the position of the book she needed to replace.

For a moment, she felt uncomfortable knowing the rest of her team was listening in on their intimate encounter, but then she remembered that Jim hadn't hesitated to encourage her to have sex with the general if that meant furthering the cause of their mission. Besides, he'd been mostly polite and gentle with her, and she felt herself becoming attracted to his strong and gentlemanly manner.

After a few minutes of her sucking his turgid organ, he placed his hands on her cheeks and pulled her away.

"I don't want to finish this way," he said, lifting her up and kissing her gently on the lips.

"Am I not doing it the way you like?" Riley said.

"No, it's not that. It's just that I want *all* of you..."

He turned her around, placing her back against the bookcase, then he reached under her dress and pulled her panties all the way down her legs. When Riley stepped out of them, he lifted her skirt, pressing his dick between her slippery thighs. She pointed the tip toward her hole and when he inserted it into her slit, she placed her arms around his neck, wrapping her legs around his hips.

This time he seemed far more interested in extending the interlude, thrusting into her slower and more gently while he kissed her passionately on the lips. Riley could feel the pangs of pleasure beginning to emanate from her hips, and she tilted her pelvis until her clit began to rub across the top of his cock. The general was a patient and skilled lover, and she found herself becoming lost in the moment, genuinely enjoying the encounter.

Who cares if they can hear what we're doing? she said to herself. *I'll give them something to really talk about.*

As the general's grip on her ass began to tighten and his grunting increased in urgency, Riley reached under his buttocks and grabbed his balls, feeling them tightening toward climax.

"Oh God," the general groaned. "I can't hold it much longer."

"Yes, baby," Riley panted in his ear, putting on a show as much for the rest of the team as for the general. "Let it go. I'm going to cum all over your balls."

When the general made one final powerful thrust against her and quivered next to her body, she quickly reached her own climax, squirting jets of lubrication down the insides of his thighs. They held onto each other for a long moment against the shaking bookcase until the general pulled back a few inches, peering into Riley's eyes.

"That was incredible," he said. "I haven't had sex like that in ages. I know this isn't proper protocol, but it feels so right."

"I won't tell if you don't," Riley smiled, pulling up her underwear and straightening her dress as the general zipped his fly.

While he inspected his pants to make sure Riley's wetness hadn't stained the fabric, she turned around to inspect the books on his bookcase. Running her fingers across the bindings, she paused at the red spine of one book.

"Mein Kampf," she nodded, referring to Hitler's famous manifesto that he'd written during his rise to power. "I've always wanted to read this."

"You're welcome to borrow it if you like," the general smiled. "As long as you return it when you're done. Every SS officer is expected to have a copy on his bookshelf."

"Thank you," Riley said, removing the book from the shelf and slipping it into her purse. "I'll return it as soon as possible."

When Riley and Petra returned home later that night, they checked the newsstand to see if they had a new update from Jim, then Petra pulled Riley quickly up the steps, eager to hear about her earlier tryst in the office.

"Oh my God," she said with wide eyes. "You have got to tell me what happened at the office earlier today. When you came out of the general's office, you were practically glowing. The whole office could hear the thumping and groaning in there. What the hell is going on between you two?"

"I was told to do whatever it took to gain the general's confidence," Riley smiled. "He seems to be taking quite a shining towards me."

"I'll say," Petra nodded. "Even *I* was getting turned on listening to the two of you going at it. Are you starting to develop feelings toward him?"

"Maybe a certain *type* of feeling," Riley grinned. "He's actually a very tender lover when he sets his mind to it. It's not as horrible as I thought it would be."

"Were you able to uncover any more information about the bomb development plans?"

"No," Riley said, pulling the general's book out of her purse. "But I was able to remove the targeted book from his shelf. Tomorrow I'll try to replace it with the copy with the camera inside."

"Wow," Petra said, raising an eyebrow in surprise. "You

don't waste any time fooling around. Speaking of which, can I get a piece of that ass too? I've been dying to make love to you all day."

"Maybe just a quickie," Riley smiled. "I should probably read at least part of this book in case the general asks me about it when I return it."

"*Fuck* Hitler," Petra said, peering down at the book on the table. "I only want to fuck you."

17

———

The following morning, Riley could hear the office clock on the wall ticking, knowing they didn't have much time left to destroy the fortress. If they were going to make their move, they'd have to act quickly to plant the camera and locate the plans. While she typed quietly on her typewriter, the other secretaries kept darting their eyes in her direction, whispering amongst themselves. When the general called her into his office, she slipped his book into her purse and closed the door softly behind her.

"You called, sir?" she said, pausing behind the door.

"I think we've reached the point that you don't need to address me so formally, at least in private," the general smiled. "Why don't you call me Hans?"

"I'm not sure that's a good idea, sir," Riley said. "The girls in the secretary pool are already suspecting some impropriety, and I don't think we should risk feeding the rumors."

The general got up from behind his desk, approaching Riley slowly.

"Except it's not really *rumors*, is it?" he said, caressing the side of her cheek. "There's not much they can do about it, since I'm in charge around here."

He pulled out the chair with the planted bug and sat down on it, inviting Riley to join him.

"Come sit with me for a moment," he said, adjusting the bulge in his trousers. "It'll be more comfortable here, and we won't make as much noise on the padded cushion."

Riley peered at the chair, concerned as much about damaging the bug as she was about fucking the general right next to the listening device.

"Is there somewhere more private we can go?" she said. "Where we can take our time and not have to worry about prying eyes?"

The general paused as his eyes darted over Riley's face, pleased to see her growing interest in him.

"Yes," he smiled. "It would be nice not having to rush, where we can get fully undressed for a change. I've got a commitment I need to attend to this evening, but I'll try to arrange something tomorrow around lunchtime. That way it won't look as suspicious to the rest of the group."

"I'll look forward to that, sir," Riley said, reaching into her purse and pulling out the copy of Mein Kampf with the planted camera inside. "Oh, I almost forgot, I finished your book last night."

"So soon?" the general said.

"I found it quite fascinating," Riley lied. "I could hardly put it down."

"Was there a part that you found particularly compelling?" the general said.

Riley tried to remember some details of the book that would be vague enough to indicate she'd read it but not so specific to expose her ignorance.

"I think it was his discussion of the early years and how the events of his childhood informed his world view."

"Mmm," the general nodded. "For me, it was his revelation about the Jewish menace and their conspiracy to gain control of all elements of society. I consider them a scourge that must be eliminated at all costs."

"He certainly builds an interesting case," Riley said, clenching her teeth knowing the general would have Petra exterminated if he discovered she was Jewish. "Shall I place the book back on your shelf? I think we juggled things around during our little tryst yesterday."

"Yes," the general said. "I'll straighten things up later."

Riley wedged the book into the missing spot on his bookcase and angled the spine in the direction of the safe, then straightened up some of the adjacent books to discourage the general's meddling. When she turned around, he was already standing up, straightening out his trousers.

"Did you want me for anything else this morning?" Riley said.

"No," the general said. "I'll look forward to seeing you tomorrow at lunch. Although I'm not sure how much time we'll have for *food*."

"I'm sure we can find some other way to satisfy our oral cravings," Riley smiled.

"I'm sure we will," the general said, opening the door to his office and glancing toward the secretary pool as Riley headed back to her desk.

Later that morning, the Gestapo major stopped by Riley's desk, asking her to join him in his office. When they entered the room, he closed the door firmly behind them, standing uncomfortably close to Riley.

"Was there something you needed, sir?" Riley said, taking a step back.

"Oh, there's plenty of things I *need*," the major smiled. "But in my line of work, I find they are rarely provided willingly."

"I can't imagine what you mean..." Riley said, feeling her heart suddenly pounding in her chest again.

"Have a seat, Greta," the major said, motioning to a bare wooden chair on the other side of his steel desk. "Or should I call you *Riley*?"

Riley paused for a moment, terrified that her cover had been blown. There were only two ways the major could know about her real name, and she hoped that it was from overhearing it during private conversations with Petra.

"Only my close friends call me that," she said.

"Isn't it a bit Anglicized for a proper German girl like you?"

"It's something my classmates at college used to tease me about," Riley lied, her mind racing a million miles an hour to come up with an explanation. "It comes from the English expression Life of Riley, meaning the good life. I guess I spent so much time talking about it, they adopted it as my nickname."

"Is that why you took a job at the southern headquarters?" the major said. "Trying to finagle your way into a better position?"

"No," Riley said. "The job just opened up, and Herr Muller thought I'd be a good fit."

"*Herr* Muller?" the major said, raising an eyebrow. "Are you on informal terms with him now?"

"I meant Obergruppen Fuhrer Muller," Riley said, correcting herself.

"It seems that you've become a good fit for him in more ways than *one*," the major smirked.

"I have no idea what you mean–" Riley said.

"Our come now, Greta," the major said, leaning forward on his desk. "I've seen the two of you outside the office, and the other secretaries have begun to talk. I know you two have more than an arms-length relationship, in a manner of speaking."

Riley hesitated for a moment, realizing the major had probably trailed them back from the restaurant, catching them having sex in the alley. It would be fruitless to deny what he already knew, only arousing further suspicion about her intentions.

"So what if we *do*?" she said calmly. "Is it a crime for two people to be attracted to one another?"

"Not a *crime* perhaps," the major sneered. "But certainly bad form, given that he's your boss. Not to mention a married man. If his superiors were to find out, he could be reprimanded, or worse."

Riley stared at the major, trying to decipher his goal. Although his job was to root out enemies of the state, the general was a very powerful man with ties to the top ranks of the Nazi hierarchy. They would be unlikely to discipline him for a minor dalliance with an office secretary, given his pivotal role in the imminent completion of the nuclear program.

"Perhaps," Riley smiled, deciding to call his bluff. "But something tells me they have higher priorities. As for his wife, I suspect she's enjoying a newfound spark in their love life."

The major peered across his shiny desk at Riley for a long moment, while a sinister grin began to spread across his face.

"You'd best tread lightly with your extra-curricular activities, Fraulein Schrader," he said, sliding his chair noisily across the floor as he stood up behind his desk. "I'll be watching you carefully from here on out. And your pretty friend Petra, too. If I uncover any further irregularities, I'm afraid your new friend Herr Muller won't be able to save you from your little life of Riley."

18

When Riley and Petra headed back to their apartment later that afternoon, they found a new letter awaiting them at the newsstand, and they opened it as soon as they got home.

Combination for the safe identified. Right 33, left 26, right 37. Will create a distraction outside the headquarters when Riley departs for lunch with the general. Petra will have only a few minutes to break into his office and take photos of essential documents. Watch your backs, the crocodiles are circling.

"Crocodiles?" Petra said, peering at Riley with a wrinkled brow.

"He's probably referring to the Gestapo major. The major seems to have taken notice of my special relationship with the general."

"I noticed you going into his office earlier today," Petra nodded. "What did he want?"

"I saw him in the restaurant the other day. I think he followed me and the general home, catching us having a fling in the alley."

"Do you think he'll report it?"

"Unlikely," Riley said. "The general is too powerful, and the major would need more than an ill-advised affair to get either of us in trouble. I'm more concerned about *you*. He suspects we're up to something, and he'll be watching you more carefully now that I've gotten close to the general."

"Do you think there's some way we can divert his attention?"

"Jim's planning to create a distraction after I leave with the general for lunch tomorrow. It will have to be something big in order to create a large enough opening. You'll have to get in and out of his office fast in order not to be discovered. I'll try to unlock his window in case you need to make an emergency exit."

"Jesus," Petra said, looking at Riley with a worried expression. "It's a good thing we're getting close to the prize. The dragnet seems to be closing around us. You're not really just going to have *lunch* with the general tomorrow, are you?"

"No," Riley smiled. "But I'll try to make it as memorable as possible to buy you a little more time."

"Well, don't get *too* attached to that cock," Petra said, sliding her hand under Riley's dress. "I've still got first dibs on your pretty pussy."

"Well, technically, our handsome captain does," Riley grinned. "But I'm happy to share the spoils."

The next day, she and Petra could barely breathe, knowing the success of the mission hinged on whether they'd be able to break into the general's office and copy the fortress plans. It would be all the more difficult with Major Hoffmann snooping around and watching for any irregularities. They had no idea what kind of distraction

Jim had planned to create, but either way, they'd have to act fast. Shortly before noon, the general called Riley back into his office, closing his safe just as she entered the room.

"That's a pretty dress," he said, swinging around to admire her floral ensemble. "You seem to get more beautiful every day."

"I'm glad you like it," Riley said, glancing outside his window. "Though I'm not sure it will be warm enough on such a chilly day. Do you mind if open your window a crack to test the temperature?"

"Of course," the general said, unlatching the clasp. "But be careful, it's three flights down to the courtyard. I wouldn't want you falling and make a mess of your pretty dress."

"I wouldn't think of it," Riley said, opening the window and peering outside for any sign of her commando team. The only thing she noticed was a long black Mercedes idling beside the large fountain in the courtyard. She pulled the window closed, then she turned around, smiling at the general.

"Do you think you're dressed warmly enough?" the General said, stepping toward the window to relatch the lock.

"I'm sure it will be fine," Riley said, intercepting him while swinging her arms around his neck. "Besides, something tells me you'll be providing all the warmth I need soon enough."

"You've got that right," he said, sliding his arm around her waist and pulling her toward the office door. "Come, I've reserved the best room at the Bayerischer Hotel. This time, we can relax while we sip on champagne in the privacy of our own room."

"Mmm," Riley purred, kissing the general on the cheek. "That won't be the *only* thing I'll be sipping."

After their car left the courtyard, Petra waited at her desk, clutching her lipstick camera tightly in her hand while she rehearsed the general's safe combination over and over in her head.

33-26-37, 33-26-37, she softly said under her breath.

The time seemed to pass agonizingly slowly while Major Hoffmann paced up and down the corridors, seemingly perturbed at Riley's sudden departure with the general. Petra put the lipstick tube in her side pocket and pretended to type on her typewriter, pulling one sheet after another from the roll while she awaited the signal from her team.

What's holding them up? she cursed under her breath, eager to get the risky operation over with.

At precisely twelve-forty-five, an enormous explosion rattled the SS headquarters, sending debris flying in every direction. While the secretaries screamed and clamored for the main exit, Petra glanced toward Major Hoffmann's office. When he rushed out and peered in the direction of the explosion in the courtyard, she ducked under one of the secretary's desks, pulling the chair toward her to disguise her curled-up body.

The major yelled for everyone to evacuate the building, walking through the anteroom to make sure everyone had left, then Petra heard his jackboots tramping down the granite steps toward the smoking front entrance. She pushed the chair out and dashed over to the general's office, breathing a sigh of relief that it wasn't locked. She closed it behind her and twisted the lock, then rushed over to the safe, turning the tumblers, following Jim's instructions.

It took three attempts to open it, and when she did, she

found a thick pile of documents stacked inside. Unsure which ones to copy and knowing she didn't have much time, she placed the documents upside down on a corner of the general's desk, then flipped each one over and lay it flat on his desk while she took a picture. After she finished, she restacked them in the order she'd found them, then placed the stack back in the safe right side up, closing the door gently.

Suddenly, the door to the general's office began rattling as someone tried to get in, and Petra glanced toward the window, realizing it was her only way out. While the person at the door fished a key in the lock, she swung open the window and peered down.

Christ, she cursed to herself. *I forgot that we're three floors up.*

Glancing at the exterior wall, she noticed horizontal gaps in the limestone masonry every three feet or so, providing a narrow foothold. She climbed onto the ledge and placed the lipstick camera in her side pocket, pulling the window pane closed just as Major Hoffmann stormed into the general's office. Ducking her head just in time, she placed the tips of her pumps into one of the crevasses, lowering herself slowly while her fingers cramped trying to support her weight.

Halfway down, one of her hands slipped and her body swung out to the side, dangling precariously above the cobbled courtyard. Fortunately, she was able to regain her balance and continue scaling the wall under the cover of the smoke from the explosion, jumping onto the ground and circling around the front to join the rest of the staff huddling next to the fountain.

A few minutes later, the major emerged from the front entrance, peering at Petra suspiciously.

"Where've you been?" he said, approaching her with a stern expression. "I haven't seen you anywhere."

"I felt sick to my stomach and had to throw up around the corner of the building," she said.

"Well, stay with the rest of the group while we investigate what happened," he said. "Some things aren't adding up around here."

Twenty minutes later, the general's Mercedes screeched to a halt in front of the fountain, and he climbed out, peering up at the smoking building.

"What the hell happened here?" he said as the major came out to greet him.

"We're still not sure," Major Hoffmann said, glancing toward Riley as she stepped out of the car. "There was a loud explosion in the courtyard not long after you left."

"Yes, I heard it all the way from the hotel," the general nodded. "I came back as fast as I could. Was anything damaged?"

"Nothing too serious other than the statue in the fountain," the major said, nodding toward the toppled bust of Princess Mathilde lying broken on the cobblestone bricks.

"Are the premises secured?"

"Jawohl, Herr General," the major said.

"Alright," the general said, peering toward the women huddled next to the fountain. "The rest of you can take the day off, but we'll expect everyone to report for duty first thing tomorrow morning. If any of you noticed anything suspicious, please report it to Major Hoffmann immediately."

Then the general turned around to face Riley, who was standing next to Petra with her arms huddled over the front of her dress.

"Will you be able to make your way home this afternoon?" he said. "I'm going to have to attend to matters at the headquarters."

"Yes," Riley nodded, peering out to the main avenue. "It looks like the streetcars are still running."

"I'll see you tomorrow, then. Be safe."

"Yes, general," Riley said, interlocking her arm with Petra's and heading in the direction of the thoroughfare.

But when they reached the street, Petra thrust her hands into her pocket, stopping abruptly.

"What is it?" Riley said, looking at her with a concerned expression.

"The camera," Petra said. "It must have dropped out of my pocket when I was climbing down the wall. We have to go back and find it."

19

"It's too risky," Riley said. "The place will be crawling with Gestapo agents by now."

"We can't just leave it there," Petra said. "They'll be looking for bomb fragments, and if they find the lipstick tube, they'll tear it apart and find the pictures I took."

Riley paused for a moment, peering back in the direction of the SS headquarters.

"Okay," she nodded. "I'll go back and distract the general while you look for it."

"How are you planning to do that? He won't be much interested in having *sex* at a moment like this."

"I'll think of something," Riley said. "Just act fast, since we likely won't have much time."

When the women returned to the front of the building, the general stopped them, pinching his eyebrows in puzzlement.

"Was there something you wanted to report?" he said.

"I just came back for my coat," Riley said, peering up the stairs. "It's chillier than I thought outside."

"It's not safe to go back inside," the general said. "Wait here while I fetch it for you."

While the general went inside to retrieve Riley's coat, Petra slipped around the side of the building to look for the lipstick case. After a few minutes, she found it lying a few feet to the side of his window, but as she leaned over to pick it up, Major Hoffmann suddenly loomed up behind her.

"Did you lose something?" he said, peering at the capsule in her hand.

"Yes," Petra said, trying to still her shaking fingers. "I dropped my lipstick case when I had to excuse myself earlier."

"May I?" the major said, holding out his hand.

"You want to inspect my lipstick?"

"Yes."

Petra fished it out of her pocket, handing it to him gingerly. He turned it over, inspecting the sticker covering the pinhole on the bottom then pulled off the lid, twisting the two parts in his hand and holding the tip to his nose, sniffing it gently.

"It's much too small to be a bomb, don't you think?" Petra said, reading his mind.

"So it would seem," the major said.

Then he dropped the tube onto the cobblestones, stomping his heel down hard overtop of it. When he picked it up, he pulled the broken casing apart, noticing the components inside.

"But not too small to be a camera."

He pointed his pistol at Petra and grabbed her by the arm, dragging her toward the front of the building. When the general saw the two of them, he shook his head, peering quizzically at the major.

"What's the meaning of this, major?" he said, glancing at Petra's ashen face.

"I found Fraulein Kruger retrieving this hidden camera under your window. It appears the explosion was simply a diversion to get into your office."

The general swung around, staring at Riley with flaring eyes.

"Did you have anything to do with this?" he said.

Riley simply froze, not knowing what to say.

"Isn't it obvious, Herr General?" the major said. "The explosion, the lunch date to lure you away from the office, their suspicious movements? They're obviously working together."

The general glanced back and forth between the two women who were staring at each other with a resigned look. They both knew the jig was up and that they'd never see their colleagues again.

"Take them inside and secure them in the holding room," the general said to Major Hoffman. "I'll be up shortly to assist with the interrogation."

Major Hoffmann marched Riley and Petra up the steps under guard, then he placed them in a small holding cell, snickering as he closed the door.

"Like I said earlier," he grinned at Riley. "Your feminine charms will take you only so far. You'll soon learn where the general's allegiances really lie."

When he slammed the door, the two girls peered at one another, shivering in fright. They shuffled their bodies together, clasping onto each other, curling into a ball on the floor.

"I guess we shouldn't have come back for the camera," Petra chuckled nervously.

"No, you were right," Riley said. "They would have found

it anyway. Once they developed the pictures, it wouldn't have taken long to put the pieces together."

"So, what now?" Petra said, quivering next to Riley.

"It doesn't look good," Riley nodded. "We both know the reputation of the Gestapo. They'll stop at nothing to uncover the information they want."

"What about your time machine?" Petra said. "Can't we use it to escape?"

"It was too dangerous to keep it on my person," Riley frowned. "I'm afraid all that modern technology is no good to us now."

Fifteen minutes later, General Muller and Major Hoffmann entered the interrogation room, closing the door softly behind them. The general had the doctored copy of Mein Kampf in his hand while the major dangled the listening device from his fingers. The general motioned for the two women to sit beside each other on the aluminum chairs next to the steel table, and he sat on the other side while the major stood next to the two of them.

"I'm disappointed in you," the general said, peering at Riley with vacant eyes. "I thought we actually had something there for a moment."

Riley simply sat still in her chair, knowing there wasn't any point in playing the game any longer.

"You *will* tell us who you're working for and what your objective is. It's only a matter of time before we get what we need out of you. We can do this the easy way or the hard way."

Riley and Petra stared straight ahead, knowing the situation was hopeless. The general motioned toward Major

Hoffmann, and he pulled his hand back, striking Riley hard across her cheek with his fist. She grunted and swung to the side, rubbing the side of her dripping face.

"It's a shame to mess up that pretty face," the general said, staring at Riley with steely eyes.

Then he turned toward Petra.

"What about you, Petra, if that's your real name? What's your role in this affair? How long have you been working with the Americans?"

Petra simply stared back at the general, curling one side of her mouth into a sneer.

Suddenly, the major grabbed hold of her neck with two hands, lifting her out of her chair and pressing her against the wall while she kicked and gasped for air. As her eyes bulged wider and her lips began to turn blue, the major dropped her onto the floor, toppling one of the chairs over. The general motioned for him to place her back in the chair, then he leaned forward on the table, turning his head between the two women.

"Surely you know there is only one way this can end," he said. "The question is, how painful do you want it to be?"

The two women looked at one another while a teardrop slowly tumbled down the side of Petra's cheek. She reached out to hold Riley's hand, and the general slammed his fist on the table next to them.

"How touching," he said, peering at Riley. "Is this how you show real affection? Are you *fucking* her, too? I'm going to give you two a few minutes to think about it, then the major and I are going to come back in here and kill one of you if you don't give us what we want. You can decide which one it will be."

20

———

After the officers left the room, Riley peered at Petra, shaking her head.

"It's no use, Petra," she said. "They're going to get it out of us one way or the other."

"Not if they kill us both," Petra said, determined to hold out to the end.

"They'll only kill *one* of us right away," Riley said. "Then they'll torture the other one until we spill what we know."

"Maybe we should just tell them," Petra said. "By now, Jim's team will have seen them discover the bugs and they'll have moved their operation to another location. We can't really do any more damage than we've already done."

"Except to reveal that we know about their bomb development plans."

"The general must know that you've already passed what you know along to the team. They're probably already making plans to secure the bomb."

"Not necessarily," Riley said. "All he knows is that we suspect it's some kind of bomb, not a nuclear weapon. They still need to process the uranium fuel to complete the weapon. If we stall for enough time, maybe the team can still destroy the plant."

"What if he carries through with his threat to kill one of us?"

"It doesn't really matter, since he's going to kill both of us eventually anyhow. But I have a feeling he's going to keep us alive to work us against one another. Just try to keep your wits about you a little longer."

T he time passed agonizingly slowly while the two women waited for the general and the major to return to the room, and when they did, their hands were sweating while they held on to one another other.

"Well?" the general said, sitting down in front of them again. "Have you decided to spill your secrets, or are you ready to watch your partner die?"

"Go ahead and kill us," Petra sneered. "You're just going to do it later anyway. At least this way, we go fast and easy–"

Major Hoffmann suddenly grabbed Petra's hair and slammed her face down onto the table, drawing his pistol and aiming it toward her temple.

"Do you really want to watch your girlfriend's brains spilled all over the table right in front of you?" he sneered, glaring at Riley. "Tell us everything you know, or we'll kill her right now."

Riley peered down at Petra, looking into her eyes plead-ingly, contorting her face into a horrified grimace.

"Don't do it, Riley," Petra said. "Don't give them the satis-faction of getting it out of us easily. I'm prepared to die for the cause. I love you–"

"Shut up, bitch!" Major Hoffmann screamed, slamming

Petra's head against the table repeatedly. "What's it going to be, sweetheart? Are you going to tell us now or later? One way or the other, you're going to give it to us."

Riley peered at Petra with a painful smile, then she looked up at General Muller, clenching her jaw with an angry sneer. When the major saw that neither woman was going to talk, he cocked his pistol, turning toward the general.

"What do you want me to do, sir?" he said, pressing Petra's cheeks down hard against the table.

The general paused for a moment while he looked at Petra, then he raised his head, staring at Riley blankly.

"Do what you have to do with her to make her talk," he nodded. "Take the other one into the adjacent room so she can listen to her friend being tortured. Maybe that'll loosen their lips a little further."

For the next two hours, Riley cringed, curled up in a ball on the floor of the next room while she listened to Petra screaming and groaning while the Gestapo major cursed next door. Many times, she thought about pounding on her door and telling the general what she knew in the hopes they'd stop torturing her friend. But she knew that would only mean the end of her suffering and the loss of hundreds of thousands of other lives. Her only hope was that they could hold out long enough for Jim to launch a raid on the enrichment plant and capture the nuclear bomb before the Germans had time to set it off.

After a while, the noise in the next room fell silent, then her door opened with the major and a squad of Gestapo soldiers standing by the entrance.

"The general has ordered us to take you to our downtown location, where we can do a more thorough investigation. If you thought this was bad, wait until you see what our specialist can do with the right tools. Your Life of Riley is about to become much less idyllic, I'm afraid."

Two of the Gestapo soldiers grabbed Riley by her arms and pulled her out of the room, following another pair who were dragging Petra down the hall with her feet dangling limp behind her. When they reached the main hall, they marched the two women down the stairs, where an armored truck waited in the courtyard. Two of the men piled in the back with Riley and Petra, while Major Hoffmann climbed in the front next to the driver.

When they closed the barred door and the truck began rolling down the driveway toward the main street, Riley glanced at Petra slumping against the opposite wall next to the other soldier, looking at her with sad eyes. Her face had been pummeled into a contorted mass of lumps and bruises, and she was bleeding heavily from the sides of her mouth and her nose.

"I'm sorry, baby," Riley said, looking at her with beseeching eyes. "Please forgive me."

Petra simply nodded her head limply as the truck bounced down the road. She was too weak to answer and too tired to care any longer.

21

As the truck rolled down the road toward Gestapo headquarters, Riley thought back to her previous adventures using the time machine. The pirate ship and the wild west had been equally dangerous, but she'd always found a way to extricate herself from a sticky situation. The time machine had never been too far away, and she could always count on it to save her if things got too hot. But this time, she'd kept it far away, fearful of it falling into Nazi hands. Now she was headed toward an almost certain and painful death.

As she peered at Petra, bleeding and bruised, she felt sorry that she hadn't been able to save her after pushing to uncover the fortress plans before it was too late.

"May I sit beside her?" she said to the Gestapo soldier sitting next to her.

"No," the soldier said, pushing Petra to the side as she slumped onto his shoulder. "The general left explicit instructions that you're to be kept separated."

"Only for a moment," Riley pleaded. "Please, she needs–"

Suddenly, there was a loud explosion and the truck

shook violently, tipping onto its side as it screeched to a halt on the road. Riley could hear the sound of gunfire outside, then the rear door of their compartment creaked under the pressure of a crowbar. When the door flipped open, Riley saw her commando team standing outside, pointing rifles at the guards inside.

"Come," Jim said, holding out his hand. "We've got to move quickly. Reinforcements will be here soon."

"I don't think Petra's able to move," Riley said, motioning toward her friend, still slumped over in a daze.

"You two help her to the van," he said, motioning to his teammates. Then his eyes narrowed, noticing Riley's bleeding cheek. "Are you alright?" he said.

"Yes," Riley nodded. "It's mostly just my pride that's been hurt. Let's get the hell out of here."

The team helped Petra out of the truck then they wedged the crowbar over the back of the door to lock the soldiers inside, bundling into a nearby van and storming off down a side road. An hour later, Riley felt the truck bouncing over a bumpy path, and the team hopped out next to an abandoned farmhouse.

"Let's get you two inside and patched up," Jim said, helping his team carry Petra into the barn.

"Will she be okay?" Riley said to the medic examining her wounds while she lay on a pile of hay.

"I think so," the medic nodded. "The wounds are mostly superficial at this point. She just needs some time and a little rest to recover."

"I'm sorry," Riley said, peering at Jim with tears in her eyes. "We failed to complete the mission–"

"You did everything we asked of you, and more," Jim said, placing his arms around Riley's shoulders. "We all knew it was a longshot. You came so close..."

"So what now?" Riley said, taking a step back. "How are we going to stop the Germans from finishing the bomb if we can't get inside the fortress?"

"We'll just have to bomb it from the air and hope our heavy munitions can penetrate the walls."

Riley pinched her eyebrows, shaking her head.

"That will be a risky operation with our airfields so far away. Plus, you're just as likely to kill the top German scientists who are almost as valuable as the bomb itself."

"I don't see any other way," Jim said. "The fortress will be heavily defended, and without the general's help, we'd never be able to get in there, let alone have any chance of escape."

Riley paused for a moment as her eyes darted from side to side, contemplating their next move.

"There still might be a way, if you can get me inside," she said.

"How?"

"You're just going to have to trust me," Riley said, not ready to tell him about the time machine she'd stashed away. "But first, I need to get back to the newsstand near Petra's apartment to pick something up."

For the next two hours, the team huddled together, making plans for how Riley would penetrate the fortress and neutralize the bomb. The plan was to use General Muller as a decoy to get into the plant, then locate the nuclear bomb and Professor Heisenberg, allowing him time to escape before blowing up the building. As much as Jim tried to resist the plan, he knew it was their best bet for accomplishing their dual objectives of destroying the plant and capturing the brains behind the operation.

"You still haven't shown me how you plan to get out of there," he said to Riley.

Riley hesitated, contemplating how to explain her improbable time machine.

"You know how I landed in the middle of the battlefield when I first got here and knew about the German troop movements?" she said. "I've got a top-secret device that I'm not authorized to share, even with you."

"This mission is authorized at the highest levels," Jim said, shaking his head. "What could you possibly have that is so secret you can't share with us?"

"You're just going to have to trust me," Riley said, knowing if she told Jim about her mysterious time machine that he'd think she was crazy and nix the entire plan. "Now, who's going to help me retrieve my package behind the newsstand?"

"It'll be too dangerous for more than two of us to go back into town," Jim sighed. "I'll go with you. We can't afford to have any more setbacks to our operation."

22

After Riley donned a wig to disguise her appearance, the two of them drove toward Petra's apartment, stopping near the newsstand. Jim checked to make sure there wasn't anyone suspicious nearby, then Riley reached under the base of the stall, pulling out her glass smartphone.

"*That's* what we're depending on to save the entire free world from Nazi domination?" he said, squinting his eyes at the strange device.

"Well, technically," Riley smiled. "You're relying on *me* to save the free world. I'm only counting on this little thing to save one person."

When they returned to the farmhouse, Riley checked in on Petra, who was sleeping soundly, then the team began preparing the explosives that Riley would use to blow up the plant. While one of their agents kept an eye on General Muller's movements, Jim and Riley went over the details of the infiltration plan one last time.

"Are you sure this is going to work?" he said, peering at

Riley with a worried expression. "There are a million things that can go wrong with this plan."

"As long as I stay close to the general," Riley nodded. "He'll make sure I get to where I need to go."

"It's the getting *out* part that I'm worried about," Jim said, shaking his head.

"Remember," Riley said, holding up her slender time machine. "I've got a get-out-of-jail-free card."

"I have no idea how that thing works," Jim said. "But I'm hoping you'll share your little secret once you manage to escape."

"We'll have to see about that–" Riley said, suddenly interrupted by a signal on their encrypted short-wave radio.

"The eagle is on the move," the agent on the other end said. "He's heading in the direction of the enrichment plant."

"Come on," Jim said, grabbing Riley's hand. "We haven't any time to spare. We've got an hour's head start on him, and we need to get there before he arrives at the fortress."

<hr>

Two hours later, they parked their car outside a razor-wire fence next to the large installation at the base of the Austrian alps. He and Riley got out of the car and used wire-cutters to penetrate the fence, then they crawled up to the main entrance through the thick grass. When they saw the general's car skid to a halt in front of the guard shack, Riley peered toward Jim and nodded.

"This is where I take over," she said. "I don't think we'll be seeing each other again after this. Tell Petra I managed to get out alive. She'll know what I mean."

"What?" Jim said, suddenly flaring his eyes. "But you said–"

Petra gave him a quick peck on the cheek, then she stood up, walking calmly in the direction of the general.

"Halt!" one of the guards said when he saw the lone woman approaching the entrance. "Hande hoch!"

The general turned to peer in her direction, doing a quick double-take.

"Greta," he said, shaking his head in shock. "I mean Riley. How did you ever–"

"You didn't think I was just going to let you finish your devious plan to build a nuclear bomb, did you?" she smiled.

"A what?" he said. "How did you–?"

"I have an engineering degree, remember?" she said. "Einstein's theory of relativity, a bomb releasing tremendous energy. It didn't take a rocket scientist to figure it out."

"And just how to do plan on stopping us?" he smirked, peering around to make sure she was alone. "You'll never even get inside the building."

"Why, you're going to *escort* me inside," Riley smiled.

"And why would I do that?" the general said.

Riley slowly opened the two sides of her long canvas coat, exposing the tall packs of high explosives that were pinned inside.

The general's eyes bulged, then took a nervous step back.

"*That's* your plan?" he said. "You're going to blow yourself up?"

"And you," she nodded, "if you don't open the doors for me. There's enough explosives strapped to my body to take you and me and half the plant down with me."

The general paused for a long moment while his eyes darted over Riley's face.

"You're bluffing," he said.

"Am I?" Riley said, pulling a detonator out of her pocket

and depressing the red button with her thumb. "This is a pressure-sensitive switch. If I release it for any reason, this whole place goes ka-boom. You've already seen that I was willing to sacrifice my partner for the cause. My life means nothing in the greater scheme of things."

"So, what are you going to do once you get inside?" the general said. "Blow everything up, yourself included?"

"I guess that depends on what I find in there," Riley grinned, remembering how the general had taunted her during her interrogation. "We can do this the hard way or the easy way. Which way would you prefer, general?"

The general peered toward the guards pointing their rifles at Riley's head, then glanced back toward her.

"Let her in," he nodded to the guards. "But block the doors afterwards. I don't want her getting out of there alive."

"After you," Riley smiled, tilting her head toward the door.

The general grunted as he trudged toward the front door with Riley pacing close behind, holding the detonation device in her outstretched hand. When they reached the double-thick steel entrance doors beside the guard shack, the guard peered at the general, unsure what to do.

"Sir, I'm not allowed to let any unauthorized people into the facility..."

"Open the door, you idiot!" the general bellowed. "I'm your commanding officer, with direct authority from the Fuhrer himself!"

The guard paused for a moment, then he pressed a button on his console, swinging open the wide gates. When the general and Riley got inside, he turned toward her, shrugging his shoulders.

"Now what?" he grinned. "Without your precious plans

for the inside of the plant, you have no idea where the bomb is."

"No," Riley said. "But I have a pretty good idea who does. Take me to Professor Heisenberg's office."

The general peered at Riley with a surprised expression, tightening the muscles in his face.

"Loose lips sink ships," Riley grinned. "Perhaps you shouldn't have been so eager to dictate the details of your operation with your secretary."

"How do you think he can assist you with your little scheme?"

"He's the brains behind the operation, is he not?" Riley said. "First, he's going to tell us where you're hiding the bomb, then we're going to give him a first-class ticket back to America. I think he'll find the perks of his job much more to his liking on the other side of the Atlantic."

"He'll never switch his allegiance to the Third Reich," the general sneered.

"We'll see about that," Riley said, motioning for the general to continue moving forward.

23

———

The general led Riley up a flight of stairs toward a large office on the second floor, and when they entered the office, a man wearing a white smock turned around, surprised to see him with an unexpected guest.

"General," he said. "Who is our guest?"

Riley pulled open the sides of her coat, showing him the pack of explosives attached to the lining. His eyes bulged, then he turned toward the general, shaking the head.

"What's the meaning of this, general?" he said.

"This little girl is under the delusion she can stop the development of our nuclear program single-handedly," the general said. "Just do as she says and nobody will get hurt."

"What do you want?" the scientist said.

"Are you Professor Heisenberg?" Riley said.

"Yes."

"How close are you to the completion of your nuclear weapon?"

"It's finished," the professor nodded. "It's scheduled to be delivered to our southern air base later today."

"Take us to it," Riley said.

Eisenberg glanced toward the general, and he nodded quietly.

The professor led the pair down the steps under the watchful eye of the security guards, past some large centrifuges on the main floor, toward the rear loading dock. Then he paused beside a large cylindrical device about four feet long and two feet wide, perched on a steel support rack on a skid.

"This is it," he said, nodding toward the cylinder. "But it won't be much good to you without the arming device."

"I don't need the arming device," Riley said, handing him a piece of paper. "I need you to leave the building now and go to this address. Once you get there safely, I'll receive notification."

"Where am I going?"

"Somewhere quieter and more peaceful," Riley smiled. "Where you can pursue your studies without interference, knowing your research will protect innocent lives."

The professor peered at Riley, shaking his head in confusion.

"You're going to America, professor. The land of the free and the home of the brave."

"Don't do it, Heisenberg," the general said, glaring at him menacingly. "You'll never get away with it, and you'll face the firing squad once you get caught."

"America already has its own advanced nuclear development program," Riley said to the professor. "Do you want to be on the side of the good guys or the bad guys?"

The professor hesitated for a moment, then Riley pulled open her coat.

"You're welcome to stay here with us, but something tells me you won't find it as pleasant."

The professor peered at the general, then back at Riley, nodding softly as he turned to leave the building.

"You'll live to regret this decision, Heisenberg," the general said. "Your kind are a dime a dozen. We'll just replace you with another nuclear scientist that will build us another weapon. It's our *destiny* to win the war."

As the guards separated, allowing the scientist to walk down the long hall toward the entrance, the general railed at him, cursing until the thick steel doors closed behind him.

Thirty minutes later, Riley's handheld radio chirped and she pressed the call button with her free hand.

"The professor is safe in friendly hands," Jim said. "Time to neutralize the bomb and get the hell out of there."

"Copy," Riley said, holding the radio next to her mouth.

"So, what now?" the general said, sitting on the floor beside Riley and the nuclear device. "You know they're never going to let you out of here."

"Not out the *front* door at least," Riley said, fishing her time machine out of her pocket. "Good thing I have a backup plan."

She tapped the front screen and the time machine began whirring and shaking in her hand.

"What the hell is that thing?" the general said.

"A little piece of American ingenuity," Riley said, smiling back at him. "It's too bad you were fighting on the wrong side, general. I thought we had something going there for a while..."

As the swirling funnel began to rise above the glass screen of the time machine, the general's eyes widened in disbelief. Riley pulled off her coat and placed it over the bomb, then she raised her left arm as the funnel began to pull her into the vortex. Just before her body disappeared inside, she dropped the detonator on the floor, and seconds later, an enormous explosion rocked the enrichment facility, raining huge pieces of machinery and material down on the general.

As she tumbled through the portal wondering where she'd land next, her thoughts flashed back to Petra. She hoped she'd soon recover and explain to Jim that she was still alive. When she landed on a hard marble floor in a large palace, she picked herself up, walking over to the nearest window, where she saw three giant pyramids in the distance.

Egypt, she said to herself, recognizing the site of ancient Giza. *But what year?*

Suddenly, a servant girl wearing a thin tunic approached her, peering at her with pinched eyebrows.

"Who are you?" she said in a strange language Riley had never heard before.

"My name's Riley," Riley said, speaking the dialect seamlessly.

"I'll have to announce you to the queen," the servant girl said. "Cleopatra doesn't like unwanted visitors in the palace."

Cleopatra? Riley thought, shaking her head. *Now there's someone I never thought I'd meet.*

———

*R*eady *for more steamy chills and thrills? Read the next exciting volume in Riley's Time Travel Adventures,* Cleopatra's Secret. *Buy direct and save at victoriarusherotica. Or download from your favorite online bookstore here: retailer links.*

Those who don't learn from history are doomed to repeat it...

ALSO BY VICTORIA RUSH

Adult Fairytales:

The Enchanted Forest: An Erotic Fairytale

The Land of Giants: An Erotic Fairytale

The Dragon's Lair: An Erotic Fairytale

Witch's Brew: An Erotic Fairytale

The Mage's Spell: An Erotic Fairytale

The Mermaid Lagoon: An Erotic Fairytale

The Coven: An Erotic Fairytale

Rapunzel: An Erotic Fairytale

The Seven Dwarfs: An Erotic Fairytale

The Land of Mutants: An Erotic Fairytale

The Erotic Temple: A Sexy Fairytale (Coming Soon)

Erotica Themed Bundles:

Voyeur: Lesbian Erotica Bundle

Public Affairs: A Lesbian Anthology

Futa Fantasies: The Ladyboy Collection

Threesomes: The Lesbian Collection

Threesomes - Volume 2: The Lesbian Collection

First Time: A Lesbian Anthology

Hedonism: An Erotic Anthology

Switch Hitters: Bisexual Erotica

Taboo Erotica: The Lesbian Series

BDSM: The Lesbian Collection

Party Games: The Erotic Collection

Party Games 2: The Erotic Collection

All Girl 1: Lesbian Erotica Bundle

All Girl 2: Lesbian Erotica Bundle

All Girl 3: Lesbian Erotica Bundle

All Girl 4: Lesbian Erotica Bundle

Erotic Fairytale Bundles:

Clover's Fantasy Adventures: Books 1 - 5

Clover's Fantasy Adventures: Books 6 - 10

Erotic Fantasy:

Pirate's Bounty: A Time Travel Adventure

Wild West: A Time Travel Adventure

Private Riley: A Time Travel Adventure

Cleopatra's Secret: A Time Travel Adventure

Bounty Hunter 2125: A Time Travel Adventure

Ninja Assassin: A Time Travel Adventure

The 300: A Time Travel Adventure

Arabian Nights: An Erotic Fairytale (coming soon...)

Steamy Time Travel Bundles:

Riley's Time Travel Adventures: Books 1 - 5

Lesbian Erotica:

The Dinner Party: Lesbian Voyeur Erotica

The Darkroom: Bisexual Voyeur Erotica

Naked Yoga: Lesbian Transgender Erotica

Nude Cruise: Bisexual Voyeur Erotica

Rush Hour: Taboo Public Sex

The Girl Next Door: First Time Lesbian Erotic Romance

Girls' Camp: Lesbian Group Sex

Wet Dream: Ladyboy Fantasy Erotica

The Convent: Taboo Sex with a Nun

Sex Robot: A Dream Sex Machine

The Personal Trainer: Getting Pumped at the Gym

The Dominatrix: BDSM Lesbian Domination

Webcam Chat: Lesbian Online Sex

Paint Me: A Kinky Bodypainting Workshop

The Toy Party: Girls Sharing Sex Toys

The Costume Party: Strapping One On

Swedish Sauna: Lesbian Group Sex

The Therapist: Taboo Lesbian Erotica

Elevator Shaft: Bisexual Threesomes Erotica

Ladyboy: Lesbian Transgender Erotica

Peep Show: Lesbian Voyeur Erotica

The Dare: Public Sex Erotica

Maid Service: Lesbian Threesomes Erotica

The Hitchhiker: First Time Lesbian Erotica

The Housesitter: Spycam Lesbian Erotica

The Spa: Lesbian Group Orgy

Parlor Games: Blindfold Sex Party

The Exchange Student: First Time Lesbian Erotica

The Hostel: Bisexual Group Erotica

The Harem: Lesbian Erotic Romance

The Orient Express: Lesbian Voyeur Erotica

The First Lady: A Forbidden Lesbian Erotic Romance

The Slave: Lesbian BDSM Erotica

The Masseuse: Lesbian Sensuous Erotica

Too Close for Comfort: Lesbian Forbidden Erotica

Naked Twister: A Wild Party Game

Lexi: The Sex App (Lesbian Fantasy Erotica)

Call Girl: Lesbian Bisexual Threesomes Erotica

Circle Jill: Lesbian Masturbation Workshop

The Viewing Room: Masturbation Voyeur Erotica

Spin the Bottle: A Kinky Party Game

The Hair Salon: Lesbian Voyeur Erotica

Tribadism 1: Girls Only Sex Workshop

Tribadism 2: The Art of Scissoring

Tribadism 3: Threeway Hookups

The Kiss: A Game of Oral Sex

Pledge Week: Sorority Sisters

Carny Games 1: A Wild Sex Party

Carny Games 2: A Kinky Sex Party

Carny Games 3: An Erotic Sex Party

Dreamscape: An Artificial Reality Game

Glory Hole: Guess Who's On the Other Side

Joy Ride: A Late Night Erotic Bus Trip

The Blind Girl: An Erotic Romance(Coming Soon)

Lesbian Erotica Bundles:

Jade's Erotic Adventures: Books 1 - 5

Jade's Erotic Adventures: Books 6 - 10

Jade's Erotic Adventures: Books 11 - 15

Jade's Erotic Adventures: Books 16 - 20

Jade's Erotic Adventures: Books 21 - 25

Jade's Erotic Adventures: Books 26 - 30

Jade's Erotic Adventures: Books 31 - 35

Jade's Erotic Adventures: Books 36 - 40

Jade's Erotic Adventures: Books 41 - 45

Jade's Erotic Adventures: Books 46 - 50

Fifty Shades of Jade: Superbundle

Standalone Stories:

The Polynesian Girl: A Lesbian EroticRomance

FOLLOW VICTORIA RUSH:

Want to keep informed of my latest erotic book releases? Sign up for my newsletter and receive a FREE bonus book:

Spying on the neighbors just got a lot more interesting...